I had to convince them that their old way of life was gone for good, and all our lives were in danger, but how could I when I couldn't tell them how I knew...

"But, Mama, the revolutionaries are not German. They're our own people!"

"That may be, but the peasants are angry about the war and the shortages, and until the kaiser surrenders, things will not get back to normal."

They'll never get back to normal, I want to say. I still don't know how close we are to the actual revolution, but it cannot be that long. Once again, I feel that sense of panic. What will happen to me then? To my new family? I know that the revolutionaries got rid of most of the nobility. I know that the tsar and his family will lose their throne and eventually their lives, but I don't know how to warn these people.

"Perhaps we should begin to prepare for the worst," I finally say hesitantly.

"The worst? And what would that be, Olga?" my mother asks, almost angrily.

"What if we lose the war? What if the revolutionaries manage to get rid of the tsar? Shouldn't we pack our things or something?"

When sixteen-year-old Julie inherits the contents of her great grandmother's Michigan farmhouse, she has no idea what awaits her—except for piles and piles of hoarded junk. However, after fiddling with an amber necklace she discovers in a locked room, she finds herself suddenly whisked back in time to the court of the last ruling Romanovs and a Russia in the midst of World War I. As the events of 1917 kindle a flame that becomes the roar of revolution, they not only touch her life and that of her new family, but force her to cope with new ways of seeing the world, her cultural heritage, and even the complications of a unique and complicated love. And how—or will—she make it back to the present?

KUDOS for *The Amber Beads*

In *The Amber Beads* by Judith Rypma, sixteen-year-old Julie inherits the contents of her great-grandmother's farmhouse in Michigan. To Julie, most of it is junk and she spends some time sorting it all into boxes to be given away. But when she finds a key, she remembers the secret room whose door was always locked. She tries the key and the door opens. Inside, she finds a necklace made from beads of amber. She puts the necklace on, passes out, and wakes up in her great-grandmother's house in Russian in 1916, where she seems to be living her great-grandmother's life as a teenage girl. Julie—now Olga, her great-grandmother—knows what is coming in October 2017. She wants to warn Olga's family, who are members of the Russian nobility, but how can she? For one, they would not believe her, and two, how could explain how she knows what she knows? Impossible. All Julie can do is play along and hope that amber beads will take her back to 1995 before the rebels take over Russia in 1917. Rypma has created a history lesson in vivid detail, giving us much more than just the events, but the attitudes and emotions of the people at the time as well—a glimpse into the past so real, it makes you think you've gone back in time with Julia. A wonderful read. ~ *Taylor Jones, The Review Team of Taylor Jones & Regan Murphy*

The Amber Beads by Judith Rypma is the story of Julia, a

sixteen-year-old American in 1995. Julie and her great-grandmother Olga were close, much more so than Olga and Julie's mother Cheryl, so when Olga dies, she leaves the entire contents of her Michigan farmhouse to Julie. Julie knows Olga was from Russia, and as she sorts through the debris of Olga's life, Julie thinks about her Russian roots, and decides that it doesn't matter where you are from, we are all Americans. That is, until she unlocks Olga's secret room and discovers a necklace made of amber. When she puts the necklace on, she is whisked back in time to 1916 Russia and thrust into sixteen-year-old Olga's life. At first, Julie thinks it's a dream, but when she doesn't wake up, she slowly accepts the situation. She is really back in the past, living her great-grandmother's life in Russia. Then, to her dismay, Julie discovers that she is in Russia in the winter of 1916, less than a year before the Bolsheviks revolt, take over the government, and kill off the aristocracy—which includes Olga and her family. How can Julie persuade her "new" family to flee what is coming, when Olga could not possibly know the future? And how can she get the amber beads to take her back to 1995 where she belongs? *The Amber Beads* is both a coming-of-age story and a cunning history lesson. With vivid descriptions, charming characters, and a solid ring of truth, Rypma pulls you in until you feel as if you are right there in the scene with Julia/Olga, struggling to survive in war-torn Russia. It takes a talented author to do that. ~ *Regan Murphy, The Review Team of Taylor Jones & Regan Murphy*

The Amber Beads

Judith Rypma

A Black Opal Books Publication

GENRE: TIME TRAVEL/ADVENTURE

THE AMBER BEADS
Copyright © 2017 by Judith Rypma
Cover Design by Jackson Cover Designs
All cover art copyright © 2017
All Rights Reserved
Print ISBN: 978-1-626947-61-0

First Publication: OCTOBER 2017

Published by Black Opal Books **http://www.blackopalbooks.com**

DEDICATION

*To E. R., for always believing I could do it,
and to my late basset hound, Anastasia,
for supervising every page
(even when she was asleep).*

"With the rapid demise and abdication of Nicholas II, Russia was a great ship with no one at the rudder, an empire utterly adrift in a tumultuous sea."

~ Robert Alexander, author of *The Kitchen Boy* and *Rasputin's Daughter*

Chapter 1

1995:

From the day she arrived in America as a bride, until she died in her sleep at ninety-five, Great-Grandmother Olga never threw anything away. Perhaps I might have realized that, but in the four years since my mother and I had moved out of her life, I had more important things on my mind than what Olga Sergeievna Kuznetsov was hoarding a thousand miles away.

At first, when my mother announced we'd be spending two months in Michigan to take care of the Estate, I tried to refuse. I had the entire summer planned, starting the last day of my junior year when my best friend Tiffany and I would hit every mall in Dallas to spend most of what I'd earned all winter working at the library part time. Then we'd fall into a routine: mornings at the pool outside Tiffany's parents' condo, afternoons hanging out at Grapevine Lake, and evenings checking out patrons' books before heading off to cruise the streets of Euless in Tiffany's new car.

We had season tickets to Wet and Wild, and weekends we'd spend there or at Six Flags. Oh, and I would celebrate my seventeenth birthday.

My mom ruined all that, the way she has a habit of ruining *my* plans with her own. Not to mention with her marriages and ensuing moves. We've lived in Euless barely two years, and I've finally *almost* started to feel like I fit in someplace. As if I'm not some extra foam piece left over after the entire Big Ben 3-D Puzzle has been put together. "A mistake by the manufacturers," I once complained to Tiffany, who really does understand because she's an army brat. But at least she has two parents—the originals, not a succession of replacement stepfathers

As the rental car curves up the gravel drive, the messy appearance of Great Grandma Olga's house towers into view. My mom used to call it "the white elephant," although to me it's always resembled a four-tiered wedding cake. But whereas four years ago I saw only its whimsical mystery, now I notice the lopsided realities. Years of settling and shifting upon clay soil have taken a toll, causing the house to tilt westward toward the corn fields. Layers of thickly applied exterior paint have bubbled and peeled, as if the frosting has melted in places and a naughty child poked it with impatient fingers in others.

Yet the house, with its rambling wings and cluster of turrets, still dominates the area—a sugary, gingerbread-trimmed confection perched atop a tabletop countryside. For the first time, I almost wish that my great grandmother had willed it to us instead of the local homeless shelter.

I find the first clue to the dimensions of our job in the garage, where I poke around while waiting for Mother to locate the front door key. There's no room in here for a lawnmower or tractor, let alone an automobile, although Olga never learned to drive. Instead, she relied on rides from neighbors, although her fear of driving meant that, after her husband's death, she had to give up going to the faraway Russian Orthodox Church where she and Great Grandfather Ivan once worshipped.

Dirt and dust showered from the ceiling when I'd lifted the heavy door, and mice scattered from beneath a newspaper pyramid. The yellowing, mildewed papers face an equally tall tower of boxes, all labeled with Magic Marker: *Jelly Jars*, *Soup Cans*, *Sour Cream Containers*, *Egg Cartons*. I open one carefully, fearing what might crawl out. Unfortunately, the labels do not lie— Great Grandma Olga did indeed save empty soup cans. And cereal boxes. And strips of used aluminum foil and cellophane wrap, each carefully folded.

Stacks of old magazines, covers welded together by

moisture, line the opposite wall. She must've subscribed to *Life, National Geographic*, and *Saturday Evening Post* for over fifty years. Cases of nails, bolts, screws, paper-clips, and even bottle caps lean against the back wall.

The front porch screen door slams, and I scramble over boxes labeled *Candles* and *Flour Bags* in order to retreat.

My mom, who prefers to be called Cheryl now, smiles, and I notice the crow's feet that only two years ago tracked an uneven path around her eyes seem fainter, as if, like footprints on the beach dissolved by the tide, they never existed. Now that Cheryl's interior design business is thriving, she seems to look younger by the day. She looks lovely, though, her sandy complexion buffed with expensive powders.

"How was Greece?" I asked when she returned in the spring. I thought her blanched face would surely disap-pear against the background of the oracle at Delphi or the Parthenon's weather-beaten stones.

"Unseasonably warm. 'Too many dead rocks,' as Fred kept saying. But he found us this simply divine villa. And of course, there's nothing quite like a Mykonos sun-set."

"Maybe I'll see it on the postcard that must be lost in the mail." I smiled to demonstrate I was joking, although my mother's silences from afar have always been a sore point.

"Heavens, Julie. Who has time to write postcards on

a honeymoon? When we did receive the news about grandmother, all the flights from Athens were booked. And Fred didn't see any point in forfeiting all that money for the villa to fly back and arrive after the funeral."

"But we could have flown up here for the service they had forty days later. You're the one who told me they hold something then for the family—and for people who couldn't make it."

"It's called a *Pannakhida* service," Cheryl said wearily. "And there is no one up in her community to organize such a thing. You're talking about Russian Orthodox rituals. And Grandmother wouldn't have known the difference, anyway."

Of course not. *Who cares about your grandmother and her religious beliefs, let alone your own daughter?* But I didn't say it, just like I don't remind her now that she promised we'd check in at a motel with a pool, not the sparser Rest-All Inn.

Cheryl bites her lower lip as she fiddles with the lock. She's chewed off her lipstick, and I wonder if she realizes it's coral and not salmon—she doesn't usually make color coordination errors.

At last, she gives up, crossing slim ankles as she settles into the swing on the wraparound front porch. "I know she kept a spare here somewhere, but I just can't remember." She frowns, jumps up again, and straightens the salmon linen blazer, now hopelessly wrinkled from two flights and a forty-minute drive.

"Maybe if we'd been at the funeral, we could have gotten a key from someone in town."

She ignores me, but I don't care. I guess I *want* her to feel guilty that we weren't here.

And Greece or no Greece, since Olga had died days before anyone found her and Orthodox tradition meant she must be buried within seven days of her death, the funeral couldn't be postponed. Not that religious rituals mean anything to me personally, but it seems as if anyone who lived that long probably deserved to have her own beliefs honored.

Cheryl waves her tiny hands at the yard, and diamond and sapphire rings flash in the sunlight. "Well, it looks like nothing's changed here."

I follow her glance to where the twin weeping willows now completely block the view of the road. On either side, sprawling lilac bushes mark property lines, although if you could see through the last of the season's thick purple blossoms there would be nothing but hundreds of acres of corn and pumpkin fields. Nothing for miles. As a kid, I resented Cheryl leaving me here more than a few days. After climbing the willows, frightening away the nesting flickers, and playing hide-and-go-seek with my great grandmother, I ran out of things to do outdoors.

Moving carefully across the porch so her spiked heels won't catch in the wooden planks, Cheryl stands on tiptoe to reach the bird feeder swinging from the opposite corner of the porch. "Ah ha! I knew it would still be there," she exclaims, proudly producing a skeleton key from the feeder's ledge. "Grandmother was a creature of habit. I'm sure the house is a mess," she warns, jiggling the lock. "I offered to hire a housekeeper for her years ago, but she refused to allow strangers inside."

The mustiness overwhelms us immediately, but within moments mingles with a familiar medley of lemon polish, cinnamon potpourri, and vanilla. It has always smelled that way, although great grandmother used to keep the windows open "to circulate God's air."

I slide the recliner away from the bay window to push open the sash, and the heady scent of lilacs begins to compete.

My eyes sweep the cluttered living and dining rooms, their decorative wall-to-wall china cabinets crammed with glassware, commemorative plates, china, and teapots. "It's hard to know where to begin."

"She was a collector, all right." Cheryl shakes her head. "Four families could've lived here."

"No kidding. And nobody, and I mean *nobody*, should keep that much useless junk. You wouldn't believe the garage."

"Wouldn't I? You have no idea how many hours I spent trying to convince her to call a junk collector or someone to cart this crap to Goodwill. Grandmother was ahead of her time in one way only: she invented recycling."

"Maybe we should start down here, with the china," I suggest. "We could get some boxes in town, and there's enough paper in the garage to wrap everything. If we clean out the downstairs, that'll give us someplace to put stuff from the other floors."

I'm starting to feel slightly excited about the task now, not to mention a bit authoritative with my mother. In all our moves, from Michigan, to California, to Denver, and then to Texas, I was responsible for most of the packing and all the labeling.

Cheryl sighs and settles into the recliner. "This isn't a 'we' task, Julie. It looks like we'll have to hire help."

"I know, but—"

"She didn't leave *me* anything, only you and the shelter. I'd just as soon get this over with as soon as possible."

"But don't you want some photos or something?"

"No! There's nothing I want here. I told her that when I married your father. I've never asked for a thing, even before she practically kicked me out."

"Mom—I mean Cheryl—great grandma loved you. You know that." I start to touch her shoulder, but pull my hand back slowly. "She forgave you for running away and marrying Dad a long time ago. She told me that a hundred times when I was a kid."

"But *I* never forgave *her*," Cheryl says quietly, picking up a cut glass ashtray and stroking its edges. "I went on with my life, and I intend to do so now."

"Even if great grandma was right?"

"Only partially. I admit I gave up on life with a pro-verbial starving artist, but your father *did* make some-thing of his career eventually. He took care of us for a long time after we divorced. And even afterward, when his paintings actually started selling, he sent money for years. Probably still would if he were alive."

"Olga loved you," I persist, but Cheryl has already positioned herself in the entryway with her hand on the crystal doorknob.

"It doesn't matter anymore. She's dead, and she died alone. That's how she wanted it. I'm going back to the motel. Do you want to come or stay? I guess you'd be safe—"

"I'll stay. Can you pick me up in a few hours?"

I choose a time arbitrarily, not knowing how much of a dent I can make in such a short period. We have eight weeks until the house gets deeded to the shelter. Eight weeks to sort through an avalanche of crap. Eight weeks to catalog whatever the auctioneer will sell. Eight weeks to decide what the shelter might be able to use and what, if anything, I want to keep.

My great grandmother, so meticulous and emotional with everything else, showed a streak of expansiveness and lack of sentimentality when she chose to leave "the contents to dispose of as my Great Granddaughter Julie sees fit."

If she were still here, I'd ask her: "Did we grow so

far apart that you don't care what remains in the Kuz-netsov family and what goes to strangers?"

CroCro

"I don't want strangers knowing our business," Grandma Olga insisted the first time I proposed a garage sale. I was twelve, abandoned here for a month while my mother cruised the Indian Ocean with husband number three, and full of restless energy. To me a sale would solve all grandma's problems: bring in added income, enable her to meet some of the neighbors, and eliminate some of the clutter already distinguishable as junk to my adolescent sensibilities.

"No sale," she repeated firmly. "I'm not having people pawing through my things and making judgments about my life. This isn't the Soviet Union. I have a right to my things. There are too many Bolsheviks in Michigan already."

At the time, I had no idea who or what the Bolsheviks were or exactly where they lived. But I did know about great grandma's obsession with privacy, a word she explained did not have a satisfactory equivalent in Russian. "But it will someday," she predicted. "One day there might even be a monarchy again. A better one than we had. Or at least a different sort of government."

I was helping her dust the contents of the old milk chest she'd had moved from the cellar to the back porch.

Now instead of holding curdled cream, its red oak shelves housed stacks of bone china cups, teapots, and salt and pepper shakers.

"Does that mean a king and queen?" I asked.

"No, a tsar and tsaritsa. And grand duchesses, grand dukes, and a tsarevich. It's part of our heritage, *devushka,* mine and yours. Yours because you have my blood in your veins and thus Mother Russia in your soul."

I didn't, though. Didn't give a darn about some faraway place my teacher claimed was once known as "The Red Menace," a place where my mother said they used to build missiles perpetually aimed at the United States. But I knew enough not to argue with great grandmother. Her passion for the country she left after the Soviet Revolution was exceeded only by her obsession with collecting.

At that time, however, I didn't recognize it as an obsession, just a quirk older people had about clinging to the past.

What I did realize was that I was one of the few people with whom Grandma Olga would discuss these things. In Olga's mind, it seemed, her granddaughter Cheryl now existed only as the mother of her great granddaughter. They never discussed anything but me—or my father—in my presence or over the phone, and I never heard my mother and great grandmother discuss Russia.

My mother changed her own name from Katerina to Cathy and later to Cheryl when she remarried the third time. *Cheryl* did not distinguish between monarchists or Bolsheviks: to her they were all Russians or Soviets—words she fairly spat out with equal force when she had to use them.

"Why don't you like Russians?" I asked my mother shortly after Olga predicted the return of the monarchy. "And who cares anymore, anyway?"

"Because they're stubborn," she said simply and refused to elaborate.

I knew my mom's parents—my grandparents—had been killed in a boating accident when she was only seven, so she had few memories of them, and that her father's parents had taken her in. Perhaps she's forgotten that her Grandma Olga must have had photos of her own parents, too, and I resolve to set them aside in case she comes to her senses. Not that my mom is normally a cheery woman, but she seems to have slipped into some kind of a funk since we arrived in Michigan.

Her grandfather, my Great Grandfather Ivan Kuznetsov, died before I was born. My mother seldom mentions him. Great Grandma Olga, however, always referred to him as "my precious Ivan" and maintained a collection of portraits of him in her bedroom. She kept the pictures in oval frames right next to her icons, illuminating everything by candlelight each evening before retiring.

∽∾∽

The pictures are still in the master bedroom, dust threatening to obscure Great-Grandfather Ivan's memory behind the glass. The portraits frame a half dozen candles—blackened icons, all resting atop a red cloth—so that the entire ensemble resembles a shrine. It's not clear who, or what, my Olga worshipped most—her late husband or her God—although I suspect her native country ranked close to both. Drawings, sketches, photographs, and oil paintings of Mother Russia completely cover two walls. Beneath each, Olga taped a placard with a brief description: *Uglich Citadel, Church of Dmitri on the Blood*; *The Kremlin at Sunset*; *Cathedral at Kolomenskoye*; *Catherine Palace at Tsarskoe Selo, The Winter Palace in St. Petersburg*. She printed all the captions in English, as if anticipating that after her death no one would be able to read the Cyrillic alphabet.

I glance at the photos sadly, remembering Olga died without realizing her dream of returning to the land she loved. She could've made a trip back anytime in the past couple years. Perhaps she couldn't afford it, or finally became too ill and immobile. Although Russia means absolutely nothing to me, I wish now I'd taken the time to find out how she was feeling and what she thought about *glasnost, perestroika*, and all the other changes in her homeland since Gorbachev had taken over, Boris Yeltsin had straddled a tank, and the Berlin Wall had tumbled.

Instead, I wrote seldom, with the exception of my sophomore year when I did a school project on Russia for world history. She'd sent me a lot of information then and even recommended some books. I learned a lot more about Russia, but had written her even less since then. When I did, I sent brief, chatty but inconsequential letters about my botany project or music collection or my latest boyfriend.

"Great Grandma, I'm sorry I hardly knew you," I whisper to the framed snapshot of her and my mom that hangs in the middle of all the cathedrals and cupolas. Great grandfather took the picture long before I was born and long before Katerina turned her back on her family. Grandmother and granddaughter are looking at each other, and I notice the resemblance in their crooked smiles, straight eyebrows, and aristocratic noses. But I don't really know the younger woman anymore either, even though my mom is very much alive and spending more time with me this week perhaps than she has for most of my life.

A tear threatens to drip from my cheek to my collar.

໑໑໑

It's this room, I tell myself. I've always loved it the most of any in the house, especially when Grandma Olga would invite me to help polish the intricately carved pine headboard and matching polished end tables. Absentmindedly, I stroke the pale wood that has always reminded me of the color of amber.

On the fancy bureau with glass drawer pulls, a collection of atomizers and cut-glass perfume bottles sparkle on a mirrored tray. Olga seldom used fragrance, but maintained a fascination for the bottles that came in all shapes, sizes, and colors. She dusted them weekly, needed or not, and let me sample a different one each time I visited. Next to the bureau, on a matching dressing table covered with a ruffled pink cloth, she arranged combs, hairbrushes, and barrettes. She used few of those either, but kept a collection of silver, mother-of-pearl, and tortoiseshell hair accessories that I used to add to at Christmas.

I pick up my favorite—a gold-rimmed hairbrush in the shape of a heart—noticing a strand of gray hair still clinging to the bristles. So many times I'd come in here in my pajamas, and Grandma Olga would brush my hair and then hers, and tell me fairytales. I'd forgotten about them, and the way she used to stroke my head with one hand and hold the book with the other, until I fell asleep in that big four-poster bed. Most of the time she didn't even look at the pages, her silvery voice spinning stories from memory. She told tales of Prince Ivan and Princess Vasilissa, of a firebird with magic feathers, and of the wicked witch Baba Yaga. To me, they were much more magical tales than the Disney ones Cheryl took me to or bought for me on video recordings.

And then I remember the secret door.

My mother and I used to call it that because Grandma Olga insisted on blocking it with the elaborate, intricately carved headboard. She never unlocked the door for either of us, and even all the years my mother spent growing up here, she admits she was never allowed inside.

"Just storage space," Olga told us, although from the time I turned six until I moved away, I devoted a substantial amount to pleading with her to let me see behind the door.

Now I push and pull at the heavy bed to unblock the door before climbing across the patchwork quilt to tug unsuccessfully on the glass doorknob. It's a wooden door with a second doorknob and large keyhole, so I assume a skeleton key must fit. I try the front door key and then search obvious hiding spots in the room.

I will find the right key or keys eventually, I know, and I smile back at the paintings on the wall.

Chapter 2

S he could be a selfish woman," Cheryl comments over enchiladas at a Mexico restaurant when I remind her about the door. "She probably keeps half the Russian crown jewels in there."

"That'd be nice," I grin, draining my water. *Crown jewels* sound valuable. At least worth enough for a down payment on a house, instead of living with Fred. I'd almost forgotten that we're supposed to move out of the rental in Euless and into Fred's house in Plano when we return. More moving. But this time Fred has promised to hire professional movers, so we won't have to lift a finger, except to add Cheryl's designer flair to the rooms.

"We could buy our own house," I suggest, watching my mother out of the corner of my eye. But when she doesn't respond, I shrug. "Too bad Olga was actually poor all her life."

"I've never believed that about Grandmother for one moment."

"Why do you say that?" I prop my elbows on the table's edge, a habit my mother abhors. But she doesn't notice.

"I don't know exactly. Only that she always saved every penny she had. Anyway," Cheryl takes a gulp of her margarita, "she refused flat out the first and only time I asked her for a loan. She never said she didn't have the money, only that she wouldn't loan any to *me*. It was right before your father left, when I was pregnant with you, and he refused to look for a fulltime job because it would take time away from his art. So instead, she invited us to come back to Websterville and move in with her, as if I could bear such a thing. She knew I'd turn her down." She glances around the restaurant, with its ripped booths and checkered tablecloths. "Can you picture me coming back here? She knew I hated this town."

I remove my elbows from the table and sip my soda. "Doesn't everyone automatically hate where they grow up when they're young? I read that somewhere once."

"You have no idea, my dear. I was just a child in the late fifties, when everyone hated and suspected Russians. It must have been harder on my parents and then grandparents. But for me in grade school it was just as bad. We used to have these terrifying air raid drills, and all my friends said the Commies were coming to take over this country—" She shook her head, as if erasing unpleasant thoughts. "You cannot imagine, Julie, because Russians are accepted now. But my childhood was nothing short of miserable."

I don't know if she is just being melodramatic, but I do recall studying the McCarthy trials of the fifties and the Cuban Missile Crisis of the early sixties.

For the first time, I can sympathize with my mother, although I can barely imagine what an air raid drill must've been like.

"I still don't get it, though. Why would kids care where your parents—let alone your grandparents—came from originally? It seems just silly." Yet I admit I was interested in my mom's seldom-discussed childhood.

Cheryl motions for another margarita, and when I ask about the air raids, she just shakes her head rapidly, the way she does when a subject is closed.

"But how did you know Great Grandmother Olga had money, let alone jewels?"

"Well, when the Orthodox Church wanted to build a new cathedral in Grand Rapids, my mother offered to make a substantial donation. Of course, the entire project fell through, since there were too few Orthodox people to sustain it. I heard about the whole thing from a girl I ran into in New Orleans, of all places, who said grandmother had developed quite a reputation for philanthropy. I nearly choked on my Cajun shrimp when she told me that."

Cheryl takes a sip from her third margarita and laughs—an almost bitter, staccato sound. She's finally ordered a full pitcher, claiming she still hasn't washed away the taste of retsina and ouzo even after all these months.

"But jewels?" I persist, stabbing at my salad. "Olga never seemed to be the…" I struggle for the word. "…the *ostentatious* type," I finish. In all my memories of great grandmother, she wore a cotton dress with a floral pattern, thick-heeled shoes with buckles, and no makeup or jewelry. "Except for her china and perfumes and hairbrushes," I add.

"Oh, I don't know. Your father always called Olga a throwback to the Romanovs, with her regal walk and elaborate hairdos. When we first got married and still visited her, she would sweep down that staircase as if she were granting us an audience. I never noticed it when I was younger, but distance gives you perspective."

I smile, wondering if she suspects that Tiffany refers to Cheryl behind her back as "the duchess."

As if reading my mind, the woman at the booth behind us approaches cautiously and then looks at my mom as if awaiting permission to speak. "Do you remember me?" she asks finally, and, when Cheryl shakes her head and carefully sets her drink down, the woman identifies herself: "Mary Vennema, from high school."

While the two of them chat—Mary enthusiastically and Cheryl with that reserved manner she seems to use in

Websterville—I smile politely. To my knowledge, my family has always been the only Russian-American one in Websterville. They were an oddity in this Bible-belt region of staunch Calvinist ministers, determined German farmers, and thrifty Dutch Reformed merchants. I guess I never thought to ask how we ended up outside Grand Rapids, Michigan, but it didn't seem to matter. Not until today, listening to Cheryl and then to her and Mary talking, did I realize that people cared or remembered that my family was originally Russian. It still seems totally irrelevant where your ancestors were born.

"I'm so sorry to hear about your grandmother," Mary says. "What a shame she never had the chance to go back to Russia. But at least she lived to see the communists losing," she continues, "although my husband believes they will rise again. It's their nature over there to follow a strong leader of some sort. It wasn't safe to trust that Gorbachev or now that drunkard Yeltsin." When I glance up and stare at her she blushes. "Of course, I didn't mean—"

"It was wonderful to see you again, Mary," Cheryl says sweetly, holding out her hand to shake her old classmate's as if the last sentences had never been spoken.

"I just wanted to say that your grandmother was such a lovely woman. She was older than the patients at the senior citizen home were, but every week she helped feed and bathe them. You'd have thought she was a professional nurse. And she did more volunteer work for the women's and homeless shelters than three women half her age."

Cheryl looks puzzled. "Really? I didn't know that."

"My son always went over to her house for lemonade and pineapple cookies. He's twenty-one now, and I saw him cry for the first time when she died. It was such a lovely funeral, with all the gladioli and roses, and—" She blushes, and flutters her hand in a bird-like wave as she turns and hurries back to her table.

I lean across the table. "Mom! Why didn't you say something? She might as well have called Russians sheep!"

"So? She didn't mean us. Not me, anyway. And no one who knew Olga would accuse her of pliancy. She was tough as nails and more penny-pinching that all these Wooden Shoes put together. Just because she did some volunteer work doesn't make her a saint."

For a moment, I stare at her, unsure if she is defending or criticizing Great Grandma Olga. And then I laugh.

Cheryl stares back and then, as if she has just discovered I exist, raises her margarita in a toast. "Remember the time Olga chased those Jehovah's Witnesses off the property with her shotgun?"

I nearly choke on my water. "And when she used to order all that stuff delivered from the hardware store and then make the guy spread it all out in her living-room and give her a sales pitch on each item?"

My mother laughs. "Not to mention the day she scared those little Girl Scouts to death because she told them 'proper young ladies don't solicit door to door.'"

"That was my troop, too. My scout leader never once picked me up after that, remember? She always asked one of the other mothers to do it if you were away. I always wondered why."

"You think you had problems?" My mother leans conspiratorially across the table. "When I was your age, she terrified every boy who walked me home. 'Who are his parents?' she'd holler out the front door. 'Do they know their son is here?'" Cheryl rolls her eyes. "Talk about embarrassing. And when I started dating in cars, she'd come right outside and go to the opposite extreme—and ask them in for tea! Then the poor guys would sit there an hour waiting for that monstrous old samovar to boil. And the whole time she'd grill them about their families and everything but their shoe size."

"And, like, you never do that to me, Mom?"

We look at each other and burst out laughing again, remembering the guy I dated that she had called a "greasy moron."

I realize that, for just a moment, Cheryl has forgotten about my age, even that I'm her daughter.

"Didn't you ever get embarrassed by my grandparents—your parents, I mean?" I ask curiously.

"I've told you the truth, Julie. I can barely remember them. The main thing I do recall is my mother taking me to Lake Michigan, and my father calling me 'Princess Katrina.' I suppose," she adds thoughtfully, "he would have been upset that I changed my name. 'Princess Cheryl' just doesn't have a Russian sound to it—and my parents seemed to be really, really Russian if I remember correctly."

"In what way?"

"Oh, I don't know. They were both born in the United States, unlike my grandparents, but it's kind of a sense I get. I remember my mother making *borsch*, for example, and singing to me in Russian." For a moment, she looks sad and I reach over and put my hand over hers. I know what it's like not to have one parent, but cannot imagine growing up without either.

"Let's order some *flan*," Cheryl suggests, and we both pick up our spoons and grin at one another.

In the morning, I will probably think I've imagined this new rapport with my mother, but in her mellow tequila glow, I savor it.

We haven't had this long of a conversation about anything besides Cheryl's travels and my wardrobe since she met Fred.

ღღღ

Todd, the college guy Cheryl hired to help me cart away boxes to the junkyard or the recycling center, is waiting when we drive up on our third morning in Websterville. He sits on the porch swing, smoking and dangling hairy legs beneath shorts. He has an unruly cowlick and looks bored. Five years ago, that could have been me waiting impatiently for great grandma to take me swimming at the gravel pit or picking blueberries.

"Sorry to keep you waiting," Cheryl apologizes.

I unlock the door and point to the stack of boxes and bags already leaning against the entryway walls. "You can start with these," I tell Todd. "Just haul them outside in front of the garage. We have a truck coming this afternoon."

It feels strange giving orders to someone older than me—two or three years maybe—but I have a job to do in a relatively short time.

Upstairs, I fold knitted afghans and patchwork quilts, stuffing them in trash bags until I can find out whether the shelter might have a need for them.

"We might have to sell the furniture to pay the long-distance bills," I grumbled, but she only shot me "the look."

I resolved to shut up then, because not only do I love Olga's furniture, but I'm planning to ask if I can call Tiffany this weekend. And talk for about two hours, probably.

Fred's already called four times: employee problems and a rescheduled meeting with the Berlin office. If I didn't know better, I'd think Fred and my mother were as close as any newlyweds, although that's what I thought before she announced she was divorcing Sylvester, husband number three.

When Cheryl returns from the hardware store with more masking tape, labels, and dust cloths, she finds me working on the linen closets—three of them, all crammed with faded towels, embroidered pillowcases, and frayed sheets.

"Remember all this stuff?" I ask, holding up a graying pillowcase decorated with candles and Christmas trees.

"Grandmother loved that homemade junk."

"I kind of liked it, too," I admit, surprised as I say so. In Dallas, Cheryl takes me to the mall and lets me scour white sales so I can replace my linens with the latest colors and patterns.

I press the pillowcase to my face, inhaling the faint bayberry scent that Olga always used in her drawers and closets. "She must have spent nearly every evening of her life knitting or sewing or doing embroidery."

"Almost." My mother settles carefully into a wicker chair in the corner of the master bathroom. "You don't have to wear or keep all that crap. I went all the way through junior high and high school without a store-bought dress or pair of mittens. You have no idea what that's like."

No, I don't. My friends and I shop every chance we get, and both Sylvester, and now Fred, believe in lending their credit cards to teenagers. And every year at Christmas, Grandma Olga knitted me a sweater, and every year it disappeared, over my faint protests, into mother's Goodwill box, in favor of imported versions. After the first few times, I dared not complain, and if Olga noticed in the pictures we sent her that I never appeared in one of her sweaters, she never mentioned it in her letters.

"She must've bought *some* of your clothes," I say, stuffing skeins of yarn into another trash bag.

"Only underwear and socks. And shoes, of course." Cheryl fingers the buttons on her violet silk blouse and frowns. "She was too cheap to buy anything nice, unless it came from a garage sale. When I went to the prom, Laura Vanderveen took one look at me and started giggling. Olga had bought my gown at the Vanderveens' garage sale, and it turned out to be the same one Laura wore *her* junior year. All those witches snickered and whispered about me behind my back."

"We kids can be cruel, you know."

"You have no idea," she repeats.

I wait for her to go on, but she eases herself out of the chair and stands. "Too many unpleasant memories here for me, darling. I'm going back to the hotel and rest awhile."

"But, Mom—"

"Sorry, Julie," she interrupts firmly. "I detest this place, and I hope you have a better understanding of why now. I'm not a 'commie,' like my schoolmates used to call me. You asked me last night what I remember about my parents, and that's something else. When I came home the first time and asked my mother, 'What's a commie,' she took me in her lap and told me, 'Some people are just plain stupid. Never forget that, Katya.' She always called me that. And she had an accent. Maybe she was the one who came over here from Russia—or actually the Soviet Union—and my father was born here."

"Didn't you ever ask Grandma Olga?"

"I can't believe I didn't, but I just can't remember now. Isn't that odd?"

"Maybe we can—"

"Pumpkin, let's not talk about this right now." Again I imagine a glimpse of sadness, but then she signals for the bill. "And besides, Fred should be calling anytime. He needs me. If my parents did, I don't recall, though I'm pretty sure they must have. But my grandmother never did, and certainly not in death."

She hasn't called me "pumpkin" in years, and suddenly I want my mother to stay here with me more than anything. "How about taking the afternoon off? We can drive to Lake Michigan and have lunch at that seafood place where you used to take me."

But Cheryl will not change her mind. She's as stubborn as Great Grandma Olga, although I don't say so aloud. "Are you positive there's nothing here you want to keep?" I ask. "I haven't found any photo albums yet, or grandma's jewelry, but when I do—"

Cheryl waves both hands in the air. "It's all yours. I

don't need her charity anymore. I don't doubt you'll find something. As I've said, she probably hoarded her money in fruit jars and then lived like a pauper. To my knowledge she never did trust a bank enough to deposit anything, but you never know."

"What about pictures? Or the religious icons?"

"I already have pictures of my parents, and as for the rest, I don't need a bunch of photographs of dead people no one can identify anymore—or of a bunch of saints. If you actually want all that crap, take it."

"I guess not." My mother does know this about me: I never keep anything around that I haven't used or worn in more than twelve months. I smile, imagining my mauve-and-white bedroom with its almost sterile, clutter-free look carefully fostered by my and Cheryl's designing sense.

Even Tiffany complained the first time she came over to see my music collection: "Gee, this whole place looks like the kind of place real estate agents and developers fix up to impress clients."

"Well, it *is* a rental," I explained, but I knew she was right.

No matter what house, condo, or apartment Cheryl finds, they all end up with a similar look when she's done: a few artificial plants, elegant candles, designer silk centerpieces, and glass tables.

But that's the way we've always preferred it—and what her clients pay her for—and it seems we've moved too often to gain an attachment to things.

"I'll pick you up around five, Julie," Cheryl murmurs, although we both know it will be closer to six or
seven once she wakes up. She hugs me for several seconds, and within moments, the scent of White Diamonds
gets fainter and high heels click on the hardwood floors
downstairs.

I think about running after her, pulling her out of the
rental car, and begging: "Just because you and your
grandmother didn't get along is no reason *we* can't be
close." But instead I keep folding and sorting, building
lopsided towers of washcloths and towels.

ฌฌฌ

It takes nearly an hour for Todd and the driver to
load the pickup. The truck service Cheryl hired charges
by the load, plus dump fees, and she plans to take it out
of the estate funds.

I brush aside my guilt at not sorting and dividing
every single thing for the recycling bins, but don't have
the time or strength to cart things from one place to the
other.

Todd has promised to drop the yarn off at the senior
citizens center and to have his father haul away the glass
jars and cans. "Do I get to keep anything I find in them?"
he asks, watching the truck topped with amber and white
lights pull out of the driveway.

"Like what?"

"I dunno." He shrugs, but avoids looking at me, and I realize he, too, must have heard rumors of Great Grandmother's hoarded wealth.

Who knows? It might be true, I sigh, climbing back upstairs to start on the spare rooms. Maybe Grandma Olga was more of a female Midas than a junk collector who lived like a Quaker. Maybe she was like those eccentric old farmers you read about, stashing money in coffee cans, mattresses, or washing machines, and then walking around acting as if they don't have a dime.

But I'm not going to go around the yard digging, although I do resolve to check pockets, teapots, and canisters more carefully. Not that Cheryl and I need money. Mother's promotion at the firm where she worked before she started her own business gave her enough to lease a great condo, invest in some bonds, and start an IRA.

Todd hollers "so long" when he leaves, and I watch him climb on his bicycle and pedal down the gravel driveway. If Tiffany or the kids back home could see that. I stifle a giggle, although there's no one to see or hear me except a few sparrows chirping on the porch.

I've never been big on these "hick" towns, which is what Cheryl calls Websterville and the surrounding area. In fact, I'm starting to get a little bored, and, for a moment, I wish I had asked Todd what he does for fun around here. We *did* have a brief conversation about

Michigan State University, where he's majoring in horti-culture, but apparently he works three jobs in the summer and had to get going.

By the time Cheryl arrives, looking clear-eyed and anxious for me to clean up for dinner, I'm almost too tired to care. "Can't we find a McDonald's someplace?"

We find one, but it's a long drive, and, for the first time, I realize how little I like Big Macs. Nor until this moment have I realized how pressured I feel, how over-whelmed by the sheer mass of Grandma Olga's things.

I'm also getting more and more annoyed with all this cultural heritage junk. Who cares if you're allegedly Greek or Italian or Polish? Everyone in the country was born to someone, who was born to someone, who was born to someone in another place. "We're all Americans anyway, you know," I reminded Tiffany when she bragged on St. Patrick's Day about how her grandparents moved here from Dublin. "So does that mean only the Irish get to celebrate?"

"No," she replied slowly. "I guess it's just nice to know your roots and all."

"My roots today are in Dallas," I told her, giving not one second of thought to my great-grandmother.

Yet tonight I dream about her all night.

Chapter 3

Not having access to friends is killing me. The phone at the house has been disconnected, and it seems as if we're the only family without a mobile phone. I'm still super bored, so on the weekend I start on the china cabinets.

I decide to sell the vases and figurines, but am somehow reluctant to get rid of the elaborate pump organ dominating the living room. Grandma Olga never played, but I know her husband did. I'm also not ready to give up all the fragile teacups with matching floral patterned saucers. I'd almost forgotten how Olga used to "take tea" every afternoon. By noon, I find myself listening for Todd and the truck. With plenty of packed boxes ready to go, I'd welcome someone to talk to.

But then, while dusting and wiping down the teacups, I find a key. Maybe *the* key to the mysterious room.

Leaving teacups and vases scattered all over the floor, I race upstairs to Olga's bedroom.

"Ah ha!"

The main lock turns and the glass doorknob appears to be unlocked.

It's as if I suddenly entered a gift shop—or maybe a church—two red, blue, and gold icons that appear much older than the ones in the bedroom, more candles, and dozens and dozens more pictures of Russian scenes on the walls.

More junk—or stuff. I cannot honestly call it treasure, but my eye catches some intriguing wooden dolls on the bookshelves that crowd one side. I know without picking one up that they are nested dolls, each nestled inside another. On the outside, someone has painted exquisite designs with shiny paints and gold trim: tsars, fairytale characters, smiling *babushkas* or grandmothers. I wonder if they're from her childhood—or perhaps my mother's—but it hurts a bit to know Olga never showed or shared them when I stayed here.

What did she do in here? Obviously it was a place that meant a lot to her, with its portraits and *matryoshka* dolls and icons and Russian memorabilia.

A rock collection fills one curio cabinet, and I try to identify some. Amber and malachite I recognize, but I'm not sure of the glittering blue stones rippled with white lines and gold-star-like markings. I know I would have delighted coming in here as a child, even though I am always so quick to dismiss our Russian heritage. But this stuff is *cool*—even to me.

In the center of a mahogany dresser stands a black lacquered box. I run my fingers over it in awe. Almost— but not quite—reverently. The tiny painted figures look familiar, even though I don't recall Great Grandma ever showing me this box. I peer more closely, able to identify a firebird, a prince, and a princess soaring through the sky. Olga would say it's Vasilissa and Ivan, the names that recur in so many Russian fairytales.

I open the box, and feel a strange shiver come over me. Inside, cradled on red satin lining and a piece of blotter paper, rests a necklace of beads. Amber beads. Lifting them out, I can sense their warmth. Even though she seldom wore jewelry, Grandma used to have an amber brooch shaped like a ship, although I haven't found it yet. But I've never seen her wear this strand of beads.

Carefully I extract it from the fairytale box and drape it around my neck.

I'm suddenly so dizzy I have to sit down. Why did she keep this hidden in here? Did she bring it with her from Russia? What else might I find?

In spite of wanting to look at everything right this minute, I'm too tired to move, so I sink into the gold brocade loveseat in the corner. Grandma must have sat here while she stared at the two icons and lit the candles. This might've been a second private church for her.

Head resting on the loveseat, I close my eyes to get rid of the dizziness. I'd hate to pass out in here, since Cheryl won't be back for hours. Keeping my eyes tightly closed, I stroke the necklace's beads.

℀℀

There are noises outside—some sort of bells—and I sit up quickly. Too quickly, because the room seems about ten times its size.

A woman pokes her head in the door, but I hear the rustle of her topaz-hued gown before I see her face.

"W—Who are y—you? What are you doing here?" I stammer, angry someone has invaded the house.

"Don't joke, Olga Sergeievna. We'll be late," she warns. "Good, you're dressed."

"Pardon? Of course, I'm dressed. What are you do-ing here?" I can't be afraid of her because she looks harmless. Probably some crazy neighbor lady who still thinks Olga is alive.

"Come, come. No one can get the car started, so the covered sleigh is waiting."

"The what?" Even as I ask, I realize that my "what" has come out as something else. Another word that sounds like *shto*. Whatever that means.

Stupid dream. I must've fallen asleep on the love seat, because there's no doubt I'm not in Olga's secret room anymore. The room I *am* in is way cool, though. Brocaded walls. Gilded window trim. A fancy wardrobe that I seem to know is called an armoire.

"Let's go, then," the woman snaps, a bit impatiently.

I wish she'd go away and leave me alone to enjoy this dream. My clothes, for one thing, are absolutely fantastic. Old-fashioned, maybe, but to my surprise I realize I'm wearing what appears to be an ivy silk dress with a low-cut bodice. I preen in front of a full-length mirror decorated with wooden cupids and seahorses and notice that I'm still wearing the amber necklace.

So that's what must've precipitated this dream. Always at night, my dreams seem to incorporate little snippets of things that happened or came up in conversation or in a book I was reading that day. This is the same thing. I found Olga's amber necklace, and now I'm someplace—maybe in a dream about Russia—imagining I'm wearing it.

Usually I don't realize I'm dreaming when it happens, but this time I do. So be it, I shrug, fingering the beads. Let's see what else is going on here.

The woman acts as if she is my mother, although Cheryl wouldn't be caught dead in a floor-length gown that rustles like satin. *"Davai,"* she repeats, and somehow I know she just said, "Let's go."

Never, never have I had a dream in which I'm speaking a foreign language, but this time I reply in what I realize is Russian: "I'm not quite ready."

"No one keeps the tsar waiting. *Davai,* Olga."

I have no idea why she is calling me by my great grandmother's name. I have no idea why I understand her. My French teacher always says that you know you've mastered a language when you start to dream in it. But except for a few words and phrases that my own Olga taught me, I've never studied Russian.

It's like time travel or something. In all those kinds of books, people instantaneously understand the language in the place they arrive. That has always annoyed me, since it seems so, so unrealistic. Yet here I am, doing the same thing in a dream.

The woman leads me out of the room and down a grand, winding staircase. A man and a girl about my age wait at the bottom.

The girl is also in formal attire and wearing a fancy fur hat and matching muff; the latter covers two hands that meet across her tiny waist.

"Mother," she says sharply. "Must we always wait for my *prima donna* little sister?"

"Not a minute longer," the man says.

He, too, looks like something out of central casting for one of those historical films about royalty. He wears a dress uniform trimmed with gold braid and nearly thigh-high black boots. I can't decide if the boots are sophisticated or just silly-looking.

Outside, snowflakes the size of cotton balls quickly cover the fur that my "mother" has wrapped around me.

Horses paw the snow in front of the massive building we just left—almost a palace, I realize—and right in front of some kind of covered sled with giant runners. Great Grandmother Olga always included sleds or something called *troikas* in her fairytales, and there was a picture of a three-horse drawn sleigh on her lacquer box, the one with the firebird. But this sled appears sturdy and warm.

This is all getting to be too much, yet I take the gloved hand proffered to me and climb inside like the dutiful daughter I apparently am playing in this crazy dream. Not crazy, really. Maybe elegant—and a little romantic. We take off with a loud jangle of bells through the snow, and I remember that winter is one of the many things I miss in Texas.

The girl beside me laughs each time our sled passes one of several enormously long automobiles stuck in drifts of snow.

Without that impediment, it takes only minutes to arrive alongside a pale red building that stretches past what I can see. Across from it, a wide frozen river doubles as a road for other sleds, some carriages, and a number of sleek automobiles that appear about a hundred years old but have apparently rammed through the snow drifts and slid over the ice. It must be colder than I realize if a river can support all that weight, I think, and then lose my train of thought as someone in a livery costume holds out yet another gloved hand to help me down.

"Let's not be late," my so-called father urges. "I

know how much Nikolai Aleksandrovich hates these dip-
lomatic receptions, and he'll want the receiving line to
move swiftly."

"He doesn't hate them half as much as Aleksandra
Feodorovna," the woman/wife/mother adds. "Her Imperial Majesty absolutely refuses to leave Tsarskoe Selo unless it's a matter of tending soldiers or honoring God."

The rather nasty girl or young woman next to me
says nothing, but if you could literally sprinkle stars in
someone's eyes, they appear in hers. So maybe she isn't
all that nasty, and she sure is a looker. Even Tiffany, who
attracts every guy in our school, would be jealous of
those auburn curls and tourmaline eyes.

Behind us, more vehicles of all sorts approach various entrances to the palace—as that is surely what this
building really is. Nikolai Aleksandrovich? Now it hits
me, what I should have realized fifteen seconds ago: that
the man she referred to is *Tsar* Nikolai, as in Nicholas II,
last tsar of Russia. For my history project, I read a book
called *Nicholas and Alexandra*, and suddenly realize I'm
dreaming about the last years of the Romanov reign. Unless this is supposed to be Nicholas the First, although my
fuzzy sense of Russian history assures me that automobiles would not be behind and in front of me in the eighteenth or nineteenth century or whenever he ruled.

And Aleksandra Feodorovna. That might be short for
the Tsaritsa Alexandra—the empress who supposedly
ruined the monarchy with her devotion to the powers of

one very strange and scary holy man, Rasputin. Even without reading the novel about the last days of the Romanov reign, I remember that name from my project.

Now, swept along with dozens of ladies in grand gowns and gentlemen in dress uniforms glittering with metals, I am excited. Imagine a chance, even in a dream, to see the Romanovs!

We make a left turn inside the palace, and climb a staircase crowded with more men in military uniforms. At that moment, I recall a sight I've seen in one of Great-Grandma Olga's magazine pictures labeled *The Jordan Staircase*. It was all white and gold, with red carpet running up the gently winding stairs and curling back upward to a ceiling that seemed almost as far overhead as the moon. The banister was also white, with scrolls of gilded designs, on either side, and huge columns near the top. White and gold figures from mythology crowned the scene. I peer up ahead of me, hoping that's where we will emerge, but these crowded stairs don't seem to promise to connect to another staircase.

Before I realize it, our little group has reached the top, and I can look back down on the ladies' clusters of gowns that resemble a rainbow curving up the staircase below me. My high school prom couldn't hold a candle to this!

As we shuffle toward what I assume is the ballroom because of all its gold, although nothing like what I saw in Olga's pictures, I notice again all the uniforms. Many men have *real s*words dangling at their sides. Of course! One of the other factors that led to the demise of the monarchy was the war: World War I. Could that be the period I am dreaming about? It seems likely, and something I think my history teacher would've loved to have me write a paper on—that is, if she would've considered dreams a valid "source."

And then I see them, at the other end of an immense—everything here seems to be immense and grandiose—room. The tsar, also in formal military dress with gold epaulets, stands stiffly in what might be considered the throne room. Four young ladies in matching gowns line up beside him.

There is no sign of the tsaritsa, whose pictures I have seen frequently: an always elegantly attired woman wearing a diamond tiara and the facial features of a pinched close-pin.

I wonder how close I will get before I awaken. Will I actually get to shake hands with—or curtsey to, perhaps—the last Romanov tsar? I shiver, and not because another uniformed person—presumably a servant—has taken my fur wrap and gloves.

I decide to think of the woman beside me as my "mother," since she seems to be playing that role in my dream. "Will we meet the tsar?" I murmur to her.

"Stop making jokes all the time," she whispers loudly, but without losing her nervous smile.

"What do you mean?"

"Don't play games today, Olga," she shoots back, almost fiercely.

Oh, so it's like that. I'm supposed to know the Romanov tsar and tsaritsa. Great. Am I also supposed to make chit chat? *Yes, dear Grand Duchess, I, too, enjoyed tea with your family last week!* For a moment, I can almost imagine such a scene: the girl behind me—my new "sister"—and I seated in some gardens watching other teen girls in white dresses strolling across the lawn.

And then we are there. Approaching the receiving line. I forget to be nervous as we get closer to the daughters standing rather stiffly beside their father. I remember some of their names—at least Olga and Anastasia, although I have no idea which is which. Am I supposed to? Am I supposed to make casual conversation with royalty I have no way of knowing? But it doesn't really matter, I remind myself. At the worst, I can make a *faux pas* in a dream, and no one can order me to the dungeon or gallows or whatever happened to rude or disrespectful people in those days. After all, I might wake up before I meet them.

It seems as if only seconds pass before I am curtseying low as if I've done it all my life, realizing now that the little boy—the one Rasputin was supposed to be curing—is absent. Noticing also the incredibly blue eyes of the tsar and one of the daughters—the color of the Caribbean I remember from the cruise on which Cheryl and one of my stepfathers took me.

Conversation does not seem to be expected, although I realize that one of the daughters said something to me and I must've answered her. In French this time. And in that brief second, I imagine she winks at me.

My mother—or whoever the heck she is supposed to be—steers me by the elbow across the room. Now I can be truly excited, noticing a small orchestra on one end of the room and tables piled with food at the other. Can you eat in a dream, I wonder? I take a fluted glass proffered to me by a man carrying a tray of them. Champagne, perhaps? I sip one, and then gulp a second glass ten minutes later. After all, you cannot get drunk in a dream.

My sister is chatting with an old man, I note with amusement. But horror of horrors, my mother seems to think I should be socializing, too. She gives me an almost imperceptible push in the direction of a young military man, but I hang back reluctantly. *What if they start dancing? I don't know how to waltz!* my brain warns. Fortunately, no one is dancing, and this appears to be more of an informal reception. Alas, though, my feet seem to move toward the gentleman—or maybe the champagne has given me confidence.

Within seconds, I am murmuring politely beneath elaborate bronze and crystal chandeliers to some stranger with soft gray eyes and a matchstick-thin mustache.

Two more young men join us and chat about the "war" before the last one returns me to my mother with a polite bow then hands me yet another glass of champagne from one of the ubiquitously circulating trays.

Surprisingly, the noise level for a room holding so many people seems muted, almost surreal. Hundreds of candles wreath the room in a flickering golden glow, giving it an even more dream-like appearance. But champagne or no champagne, I can tell that the mood—and even the music—are subdued, and I continue to catch snatches of conversation about the war.

"His imperial majesty will be returning to the front in the morning," a voice behind me says. It is my dream "father," who has not remained with us since we left the receiving line.

"And are you going with him?" I ask curiously. Now again—for some odd reason—we are speaking French instead of Russian. Perhaps we made that switch when we arrived, but I realize that I am most certainly *thinking* in English.

My father looks kindly at me. "*Oui, ma cherie*, I'm afraid I am, as I've told you repeatedly. There's nothing to be done for it. Your mother understands, but you don't seem to. You're seventeen now, a young lady, and must accept the inevitable."

"I do," I mutter, ignoring the fact that somehow I skipped my birthday. "I was just asking. Who's winning at the moment?"

A look of almost physical pain crosses his handsome features, making his mustache curl oddly. "The kaiser, I fear, has the upper hand currently. But his majesty assumes he can reverse that. If only he hadn't taken command himself." Seeing my puzzled look, he puts his fingers to his lips and frowns at me. "Not a word, *ma cherie*. You did not hear that from me."

I don't know what to say to that, but recall from my project that the tsar assumed command of the Russian Army near the end of the war. Well, maybe not the end of the war, but near the end of the monarchy. I glance at my father sympathetically, wondering how I dare ask what I want so desperately to know. "How long has it been now, *Papa*?" I use the word hesitantly, but he doesn't seem surprised.

"Since he's been in command—or how long since I've known about the commission?"

"No, how long has the war gone on?"

"Well, let's see. The archduke was assassinated in 1914…"

"So that means it's been…" I hold my breath.

"Over two years, of course." He chuckles. "Did your tutors neglect math that badly?"

It's 1916. Okay, now I know. But whether it is supposed to be late winter in that year, meaning the beginning of 1916, or early winter of the next—meaning almost 1917—I still have no idea. Perhaps it doesn't matter, although I remember that the Revolution took place in 1917. My pretend family might not even live through it. I feel a pang of guilt, in spite of suspecting I will forget them when I awaken.

The reception seems to be winding down. My sister sulks, complaining in my ear for the second time that, due to the war, there continue to be no balls or formal events.

As if by magic, a liveried court servant appears with the gloves and stole I wore when I arrived. We walk slowly down the same staircase, and outside into a star-splattered, yet now snowless night. Again, as if magically, the covered sled we arrived in pulls up to where we exited.

"That was wonderful!" my sister gushes. "I know this was only a reception, but it's been so many years since there has been a formal event at the palace. Since I was only thirteen, I think."

"This was not a formal court event, my dear," my mother corrects her. "It was an impromptu reception."

I nearly bite my tongue to keep from demanding, "If this wasn't *formal*, what is?"

We return to the house or palace or whatever it was we left, quickly, the horses' harnesses jangling loudly. Now, perhaps, I can go to bed and awaken back at Grandma Olga's.

Beside me, my sister chatters happily, as if she hadn't treated me almost like an enemy only hours ago. I barely listen to her as she rambles about some lieutenant and what some countess or duchess said or wore.

Back in my "room," a servant shows up to help me out of the green gown. I'm wearing something resembling old-fashioned bloomers when she tries to tuck me into a huge four-poster bed, and I slowly remove the amber necklace and place it beside the wash basin near the head of the bed. A hasty examination of my naked body in the mirror assures me that I am still Julie, no matter what people in this place seem to think.

Whether I have had way too much champagne or am just exhausted from the pretend ball, I fall asleep almost immediately.

Chapter 4

This should be my room. No, Olga's secret room. Yet sunbeams piercing the open space between heavy damask curtains illuminate the same space where I went to sleep. I groan. How long can a dream last? I've got things to do. Olga's house to pack up, and Cheryl coming to get me soon. I need to wake up and not waste the afternoon asleep on Olga's love seat playing with amber beads. The beads, reassuringly, are where I left them, and I crawl out of bed to rinse my face in the old-fashioned wash basin painted with roses. For the first time, I'm genuinely nervous. Never before have I had a dream during which I go to sleep and awaken. Perhaps—I allow my mind to play with the idea for a moment—perhaps something has happened to me and I'm unconscious or in a coma. On the other hand, what if somehow I've *actually been* transported to the past? The idea makes me vomit, which I promptly do in the porcelain bowl hidden beneath a wooden lid.

My sister, dressed in a gray ankle-length dress and a white apron, dances into the room in a mock waltz. "You're up, at last!"

"At last," I murmur crankily. Larissa. That's her name, I suddenly remember. Or maybe I learned it last night or whenever the earlier part of my dream took place. Because if it isn't a dream—I shudder.

"Hurry up and get ready."

"For what?" People always seem to be in a hurry to get somewhere in this place.

"For the hospital, of course."

"Who's sick?" I start to look for a closet where my clothes should be, but in trots another servant. It's as if every time I tell myself I want or need something, it appears.

"No one, silly girl. We're working in Tsarskoe Selo today. With the recovering soldiers." Larissa removes the hangered gown from the woman hovering over me and replaces it with a dress identical to hers. "You don't want to wear the chiffon at the hospital. Remember all the blood last time?"

"Blood?" My voice rises at least an octave. Of course, that makes sense. If I'm actually in a hospital bed myself, it figures that I would dream of one.

In spite of my panic, though, I'm starting to get quite annoyed. I *will* myself to wake up, to see Cheryl's face in its motherly guise. Imagine her leaning over trying to awaken me from this coma. Perhaps on the way back to the hotel we had a car accident that I cannot remember. That would explain a lot, especially since Russia and Russians have been on my mind since we arrived in Michigan.

"Since you're moving so slowly, can you just go without breakfast?" Larissa asks impatiently as I start to follow her out of "my" room.

"No problem." I shrug, and she gives me an odd look.

This morning we climb in a sleek, huge black car. En route to some place or other, I crane my neck and try to figure out where I might be. More like *when*, I think worriedly. No one I ever knew would be caught dead in such an ugly, old-fashioned dress, and this car resembles something I've seen in a film about Bonnie and Clyde.

The car rumbles along a wide avenue lined with mountains of snow and broad facades of buildings that must be hundreds of years old.

Whether they are shops or palaces, I'm not sure, but they are painted in a fruit bowl of colors: cantaloupe, banana, blueberry, lime, tangerine. Statues from mythology cover some of them, and I gasp aloud at the sight of one magnificent raspberry building that stands where a canal and a bridge meet.

Larissa follows my gaze. "Did you see something? Is the Empress Mother at her palace?"

"The red building? Or the yellow one?"

She gives me another of her "looks," as if I'm too stupid for a response. Fortunately, she forgets about my apparent awe of the surrounding city and starts chattering away again. I might as well have Tiffany with me, so I only half listen.

"I so love Nevsky Prospekt," she says enthusiastically. "It's much more grand than any street anywhere else, don't you think?"

"Mmmm," I grunt.

"Just think," she goes on, her voice turning a shade less enthusiastic. "Bucharest must be a nightmare, with all the nasty Germans taking over their palaces and squares. I cannot imagine if what just happened there happened here in Petrograd. I do so hope the musicians who play that wonderful gypsy music at the palace don't have to return and fight."

Now she has caught my attention. "Petrograd? Is that where we are?" I blurt out.

"Quit being a pain, Olga. No one else likes the fact that the tsar changed our precious Petersburg's name to Petrograd, either, but you don't have to keep complaining about it. I do, however, miss the German bakeries. The Dutch really know nothing about good pastry."

Pastries? What the heck is she going on about now? As if sensing my confusion, she explains patiently. "Remember what happened to the German pastry shop owners at the beginning of the war?" She sighs heavily, looking out at groups of soldiers, some limping, who seem to be waiting for streetcars or some conveyance to pick them up. "It could be worse. They haven't come into our music shops and tossed German pianos through the glass windows, the way they did in Moscow."

I let her continue, but am too confused to respond to any more of her disturbing comments. This is all becoming too realistic. Soldiers? Missing pastry shops? Flying pianos? Obviously, we're at war with the Germans—that much I've already figured out—but the incredible detail of this dream makes me nervous.

Or is there yet another possibility? No coma, no dream, but another reality. Sure, I've read about parallel universes and time travel, but no one *really* travels back to the past. But no dream has ever felt like this, so multidimensional and moving in excruciatingly slow, realistic time. *Was* it possible? And if so, how could it have happened? And how do I get back? My stomach once again churns at the thought, and my head suddenly aches.

The car, which I think of almost as a limousine due to its enormous front hood and spacious interior, has slowed to a crawl. In spite of all my worrying, I begin to notice what I hadn't paid too much attention to before: the people. Other women in gray dresses move swiftly up the street, almost invisible in the midst of hundreds and hundreds of gray military uniforms. Behind them, closer to the fruit-hued palaces, everyone seems to be standing in lines that stretch as far as I can see. Here and there, a man hobbles along with a crutch or sinks onto the sidewalk.

"What are the lines for?" I ask Larissa.

"Food, oil, bread, who knows?" She shrugs. "Mama said we'll get our supplies just fine, but apparently this ridiculous war has caused rationing for the peasants."

"All those people are peasants?" What a word, I think. Apparently, I'm too rich, or too educated, or just too lucky to be lumped into that category. The lines remind me of those I've heard about outside exclusive bars and clubs in Dallas, although even the non-alcoholic ones have bouncers who select only the best dressed to enter.

"Peasants. Workers. No difference," Larissa says.

I glance at her face, but it has not altered its usual calm countenance. Apparently, Larissa has no sympathy for the lower classes, being comfortably ensconced in the upper. Nobility, I correct myself. I must be a noblewoman. Watching the weary faces on the sidewalks, I admit I don't mind.

The car coming to a standstill interrupts my thoughts. Our driver twists his head in our direction and apologizes, although he can do nothing to move forward. In the middle of the street, between what I had thought were snow banks—but now reveal themselves as mounds of garbage—stand dozens of people holding signs: *Down with the German Bitch! Justice for Workers. Bread or Revolu-*

tion. Light our Lamps or We'll Light the Palace. A few signs bear obscene drawings of the empress and a face I recognize as a likeness of Rasputin, labeled the *Mad Monk.*

"My God!" Larissa breathes next to me, clutching my arm. She leans forward. "Misha, are we in any danger?"

"I don't believe so, miss," he replies, although he sounds far from confident. "Since most of the factories have shut down due to the coal shortage, too many people have too much time on their hands."

Beside the car, a soldier on horseback rides along yelling. He fires a shot into the air, and both Larissa and I duck onto the floorboard. We hear more shouts and another shot. Within, minutes the car creeps forward again, and we pop back up.

Now I am shaking. But how can one get shot in a dream? Surely, I am invincible. At best, I might awaken now. Alas, but the car still creeps slowly up the avenue, past more piles of trash and snow, more lines, and hundreds more armless, handless, and legless soldiers.

"I'll drive you all the way to Tsarskoe Selo," Mikhail says loudly over the noise of more rioters on the side of the street. "The trains will be too crowded—and dangerous. If they're even running, that is."

At last, we are off the avenue and speeding through countryside. Here, too, soldiers straggle along the road, although they pay no attention to us.

Larissa has regained her spirits, apparently, and starts complaining about everything. "It's simply not fair we cannot have a Christmas tree this year. The Empress has allowed her servants to have one, after all. And they probably eat well at the palace, unlike their families. It's all getting to be too much—having to skimp on butter and cheese and heat. Did you feel how cold the room was last night? Papa won't even let us add logs to the fireplaces anymore, although now that he's left, Mama will. And these ugly nursing uniforms. Can't someone design something with some color?" She plucks at the hem of her dress, and I pay attention to the red cross stitched on her dress for the first time. On both our dresses.

"Where are we going—exactly?" I ask.

"To Feodorovsky Gorodok, of course. The hospital sponsored by grand duchesses Maria and Anastasia. Not that they don't have plenty of room at their own Alexander Palace, but I doubt they would want to *live* with all those filthy-looking soldiers rather than just next door to them. Except for the officers, who are ever so handsome." Larissa giggles. "Yes, yes, I know I have a fabulous boyfriend, but I can still look!" She leans forward again. "Misha, would you mind detouring past the Catherine Palace? I so love to gaze upon it."

"I don't know, Miss Larissa."

But a few minutes later Larissa apparently gets her wish, as we cruise slowly past the most phenomenal building I've ever seen or even imagined: a robin's egg blue baroque facade frosted with white moldings and crowned with glittering golden cupolas. Through the ornate black fence adorned with golden trim and double-headed golden eagles, we glimpse snow-capped fountains, statues, gardens, and tiny buildings. They all form a backdrop for a formal entrance to the grandiose palace. "Ooh. Isn't it heavenly?"

"It is!" I agree excitedly, but before I can absorb it all, we are passing a bevy of guards and soldiers surrounding a huge lemon-hued building that I presume must be the Alexander Palace, the home of the Romanovs.

A moment later, we make a turn by a lake, and suddenly approach one of the massive gates guarding what appears to be a small medieval fortress. This must be Feodorosky Gorodok, which forms a complex of crenellated walls, peaked and tent-shaped roofs, barracks, and covered porches and walkways. An elaborate church crowned with a golden cupola and fanciful stone carvings—all surrounded by several buildings in various stages of construction—completes the elaborate stone cluster.

We immediately spot several other women in matching gray or white dresses, automobiles that appear to be ambulances, and a half dozen trucks crowding the grounds.

Following Larissa into a gray stone building marked *Convalescent Home #17*, I smooth out my uniform. As unsure as I am what to expect, I am fairly certain I will not enjoy it one bit.

Inside, several small wards house reclining soldiers, several tables, and a large icon on each wall. Everything appears fairly quiet, and we are assigned to a small ward with a handful of white metal beds. One "nurse" is reading to a soldier, and another plays cards with two who appear to be feeling well. For a moment, I experience relief. I can certainly handle this.

Unfortunately, our duties appear to require more training. My heart sinks as a nun passes us a stack of bandages.

A hand reaches out as I pass the first bed, and it is all I can do not to shake it off nervously.

"Please."

The man's voice stops me, and I struggle not to shudder as I force a "hello" and a smile. In spite of the convalescent home's cleanliness, the stench of sickness occasionally mingles with disinfectant and something awful I've never smelled before.

I know immediately I want to go home. Or back to the strange home I just left if I cannot get back to Grandma Olga's.

Larissa hands me a cup and a bottle of water. Another lady in gray beckons to us, and before I know it, we are directed to a patient in the corner. I follow Larissa's lead, offering sips of water to him and eventually the others who sprawl on the beds. Some welcome us with smiles, but others mutter to us or themselves and a few whine softly.

At first, I don't want to know what I'm supposed to do with the bandages, but then suddenly I do. I'm supposed to change the ones on the wounds of some of the men, and I realize that somehow I know how to do this already.

Gangrene. That has to be the awful smell, and it's certainly the fate of two of the soldiers on this ward. They look so young and so miserable I forget about myself. Instead, I begin to move more efficiently from bed to bed, trying not to think about germs and contagious diseases. After all, if I were one of *them*, I'd want someone to take care of *me*.

Most of the soldiers want to talk, and I try to listen without staying too long at any one bed.

"What will happen to me?" one asks, as I change the bandage on the stump where his hand used to be. I can see beneath the sheet—one of the few provided—that he has already lost both legs. I struggle against the urge to throw up yet again, and am grateful I missed breakfast.

"You'll be fine," I say encouragingly.

"You don't understand. It will never be fine." He waves his hand—his only remaining limb—around the room. "This is all I have now, and they will release me soon. What can I do? I cannot go back to my wife and children. I cannot plow our fields or plant or—" His shoulders start to shake and, in a moment, he is sobbing loudly. I hold his head and murmur things. I don't know what they are, and it probably doesn't matter. How can I, an almost seventeen-year-old who lives a life of swimming pools and shopping malls—and now palaces and receptions with the tsar—relate to what this man's life has become?

I gently remove my hand from his shoulder and move to the next bed, trying not to weep myself.

By the time we leave, we've worked two more wards, and I feel more confident of my nursing abilities. The soldiers seem to have stopped murmuring so much, and when several crack jokes, I find myself able to joke back easily. It is a good feeling in many ways, and as we climb into Mikhail's waiting car, I begin to appreciate all Olga's volunteer work. Still, I am weary and somewhat depressed at everything I've seen today.

"Alas, it won't be so easy and pleasant next week," Larissa says as we head back toward Petrograd.

"What do you mean?"

"You know. This is just so much more—well, satisfying. Even more relaxing than the large hospitals. But I am disappointed that neither of the grand duchesses was there today."

I don't know what to say to that, since *I* don't expect to be *here* next week.

Yet a tinge of nervousness takes over as we re-enter the city, where pedestrian traffic far outnumbers cars, horses, and carriages. I stare at the soldiers this time, noting how many legless ones scoot along on their hands or just sit silently on the corners holding out hats or cups for coins. The lines for food and other necessities elicit no comment from either of us this time, and I bleakly wonder if, in spite of my sympathy for the wounded soldiers earlier, I am starting to become immune to the suffering. Thankfully, we pick up speed as we near the Neva River and are unimpeded by striking workers or protestors.

Back at the "little palace," as I think of my grandiose new home, I let the maid draw me a hot bath in a claw foot tub. I almost ask this one's name, but somehow don't care. I *want* to be coddled and waited on. I don't *care* if I have servants.

In the bubble-filled tub, I examine my body more carefully. There is the scar on my knee I got cutting myself while shaving. There's the same mole under my right arm that I've always had. My breasts and nipples look and feel the same: nicely rounded and firm.

It makes no sense that everything about myself would be the same, yet everyone *sees* me as Olga. I don't seem to have inherited her body or her face, but still I feel trapped in her identity. I towel off slowly, reluctant to continue this "charade," and trying to suppress my fear.

A half hour later, dressed in a violet chiffon "tea gown" trimmed with lace, I descend to our drawing room or parlor. Apparently, it is tea time, and I wait impatiently as my so-called mother pours me a cup and then offers a tray of scones, pastries, and sandwiches. A few hours ago, I'd have thought food would make me vomit yet again, but the peace and elegance of the setting calm me.

We are not, however, destined to be alone. Tea time soon becomes as crowded and chaotic as the Mad Hatter's tea in *Alice in Wonderland*. Ladies—mostly mothers with super thin-waisted daughters—arrive and depart, each imparting the latest gossip as they sip tea and munch from rapidly diminishing platters of cakes. I stare in fascination at the array of hats, some resembling small boats in size and shape and all trimmed with combinations of feathers, lace, and flowers.

Boiling and bubbling in one corner, a huge silver samovar seems to provide endless tea. I know it's not the same one Great Grandma Olga has in her dining room, but I check to be certain.

A few ladies and their daughters try to chat with me, but by the third cup, I find myself too exhausted to respond with more than slight nods and polite answers.

Most of the talk seems to be about the war, although occasionally someone mentions the revolutionaries, fairly spitting out the word. "If only the tsar would do something," seems to be the common refrain, although no one offers a suggestion as to what that might be.

Rasputin's name gets bandied about, in tones ranging from awe to disgust. Every other sentence about him starts with "I hear he..." followed by some fantastic or revolting incident. I want to pay closer attention, but keep yawning.

At last my "mother" shows some concern and sends me upstairs, where a maid relieves me of my gown and tucks me into bed. "Should I awaken you for dinner?" she asks.

I cannot answer, though, as I am crying silently. If I am indeed in 1916, how in the world will I ever get back to 1995?

Chapter 5

I awaken in darkness, except for a few candles burning in wall sconces. Perhaps—but no, this is yet
again the same room I fell asleep in, and I am wearing the same half-slip, half underwear I was wearing
then. Moving to the window, I stare out at dim lights and
hear a silence that tells me it is not even close to morning.
My room overlooks a canal, but tonight no boats ply its
waters.

It must be true, then. I have to face the fact that
somehow I am stuck in the past. How I got here or why
or how I will get back home I have no idea.

Although sick to my stomach, I know I must fight
my terror.

Grabbing the amber beads from the dresser, I start

stroking and rubbing them. That's what I was doing when I "arrived" in this time and place, so surely they must be the key to my return.

Get me home! I plead.

Nothing happens.

Striving to recall all the time travel novels I've read, I realize that most end with the main character back in the present. In the meantime, I can take comfort in that fact and make the best of things. I struggle not to think of Cheryl, or Tiffany, or the Great Grandmother whose name I now appear to share. But I am not Olga, I tell myself, admitting at the same time that I know almost nothing about her life in Russia. Although Olga talked about Russian culture frequently, she never mentioned her own childhood, and I realize I have no idea when and how she came to America. Was she a young woman, as I presumed? Truly a bride? Or an adult, married or not?

I light the fancy kerosene lamp in the room and stare at myself once again. I look exactly the way I always have: shoulder-length brown hair with reddish highlights, thin eyebrows, and blue eyes with thick lashes in an oval face, and a mole near my hairline. So how could anybody believe I am Olga? Did—or do—we resemble each other that much? Why doesn't anyone notice I am *not* her?

Questions about what might be going on in my absence from the present I refuse to ponder anymore tonight.

Relieved for now that I still have my old face, I

crawl back into bed, saying fourteen silent prayers that I will awaken this time in Grandma Olga's secret room.

⋯⋯

Instead, a maid awakens me, handing me yet another lovely gown to wear. I swallow my disappointment that I am still here, and move through the corridors in search of the smells of sausage and baking bread, hungry in spite of my fears, until I discover the dining room and breakfast. It is only the three of us, and mother seems unable to talk of anything but father and the war.

"I do hope he's going to be all right. I hear such dreadful things from the front," her voice trembles as she slathers her bread with marmalade. I nod politely, and, having missed basically all three meals yesterday, gorge myself on sausage and tiny crepe-like pancakes topped with generous dollops of sour cream. *Blini*, I somehow know the pancakes are called. There is very little butter on the table, and I remember what Larissa said about rationing.

The day seems to last forever. In another room filled with what I'd consider antique furniture, my mother hands me a ball of yarn and a basket filled with knitting needles, thread, and more yarn. Apparently, I am supposed to be knitting, something I've never done—or had the slightest desire to do—in my life. I hold the needles awkwardly at first, and just the way it happened at the hospital, I suddenly find that I *do* know what to do with them.

We spend all morning knitting, although I have no clue what we are supposed to be making. Mother switches to embroidering on a beautiful silk cloth, and Larissa starts rolling what appear to be bandages—the same kind we used at the palace hospital. Apparently, this is how we are to spend the day, or most of it. Now I have a suspicion where Grandmother Olga picked up her sewing and knitting addiction.

In the afternoon, we eat yet again. It's a sumptuous spread of food that not only makes a mockery of the shortages outside these walls, but makes me question how I will continue to fit into all these elegant gowns.

Larissa plays the grand piano—apparently, not a German one—for us, but I'm so enthralled with the elaborate carvings on it that I barely listen to the music.

"Not that one," Mother interrupts when Larissa starts a familiar tune. "No Beethoven. No German or Austrian musicians, please."

"But, Mama—"

"It's not proper, with your father out fighting those people. We're already forced to give up so much for this war. I can't even go into the streets anymore without being accosted by soldiers and revolutionaries."

"But, Mama, the revolutionaries are not German. They're our own people!"

"That may be, but the peasants are angry about the

war and the shortages, and until the kaiser surrenders, things will not get back to normal."

They'll never get back to normal, I want to say. I still don't know how close we are to the actual revolution, but it cannot be that long. Once again, I feel that sense of panic. What will happen to me then? To my new family? I know that the revolutionaries got rid of most of the nobility. I know that the tsar and his family will lose their throne and eventually their lives, but I don't know how to warn these people.

"Perhaps we should begin to prepare for the worst," I finally say hesitantly.

"The worst? And what would that be, Olga?" my mother asks, almost angrily.

"What if we lose the war? What if the revolutionaries manage to get rid of the tsar? Shouldn't we pack our things or something?"

"You act crazier every day," my sister says mildly. "The tsar is God's anointed one. Nothing will happen to him."

"And as for the war," my mother announces firmly, "we will prevail against the kaiser. Too many countries are involved in fighting him now. This packing business is nothing but nonsense. No one is going anywhere."

I give up then, at least for the moment. "Are we going out today?" I ask hopefully.

"Of course not. It's way too dangerous right now," my mother insists.

Larissa's beautiful head snaps up. "But, Mama, you promised we could go to the dressmaker's. To Madame Olga's shop."

Mother sighs. "Perhaps later this week. Can't you hear the rioters along the canal? Petrograd is not a place for young ladies of the nobility right now. Even Mikhail cannot guarantee your safety. It's bad enough you insist on going to the hospital every week."

"The soldiers need us, Mama," Larissa points out calmly. "You know that. And even the Empress and all four of the grand duchesses go."

"They only need to cross the Alexander Palace grounds and park to get there," mother points out firmly. "They are not forced to travel several kilometers through these awful streets. The garbage just reeks, and the strikes show no sign of ending."

I listen, but say nothing. Mother is right about the danger, though, as we saw with our own eyes. Still, it would be lovely to get out of this house and do something. Anything. Sewing is incredibly boring, even if I have managed to demonstrate that I have the skills to do it.

Be careful what you wish for, I tell myself an hour later. Apparently, Larissa and I have a tutor, and I am supposed to be studying English—at which, of course, I excel—and Latin, at which I am lost. After two hours of conjugating verbs and earning the stern criticism of a Monsieur Bordet, I am ready to go back to sewing. At least I've dazzled monsieur with my English.

Evidently, I'm already supposed to know the language in which he addresses us and feel grateful for three years of high school French. When I spoke it at the Winter Palace, I recall, I seemed much more fluent that I had thought I was.

Thankfully, the lessons come to an end and Monsieur Bordet departs, but only because it is tea time. I feel a sense of *déjà vu* as my mother pours tea and a servant passes around more pastries. Already my gown feels tighter. Once again, we play host to a constant parade of ladies and their daughters, who arrive with calling cards and the usual gossip about the royal family and the war.

"The empress and her daughters have gone to Novgorod to inspect the hospitals there," a duchess announces, adding, "Thank God she is away from the *starets*. That man will be the ruin of Russia!"

This is followed by a lengthy debate about the merits versus the horrors of the exploits of the holy fool—the *starets*—aka Rasputin. According to which woman speaks, he is either the devil incarnate or God himself.

Once again, I think of the Mad-Hatter's tea, how it is tea time all the time, and resist the urge to laugh aloud, lest the ladies find me absolutely insane. I *do* feel like Alice, though.

I have apparently fallen down some kind of rabbit hole and am now lost in a place with kings, queens, soldiers, and gardens. A place where nothing seems to make much sense. A place I cannot seem to escape. If only they were all just a deck of cards.

ℰ⁓ℰ⁓

Nights, too, seem dull, as we play board or dice games or work on putting puzzles together.

On Sunday, I get my wish to leave the house. Tanya, the maid who handles our dressing, presents me with a teal gown and a shawl with a matching veiled silk hat. Apparently, we are to go to church.

The car is refusing to run again and fuel has soared in price, so our horse-drawn sled rumbles over cobblestones and then through mud and potholes as we take a short ride in the bitter cold to a cathedral I know I've seen in pictures. It is called St. Isaac's, and I tremble with the beauty of it. Huge malachite and lapis lazuli columns reach toward a series of domes richly painted with biblical scenes and a golden-haloed Jesus.

My mother and sister cross themselves repeatedly at each icon: three fingers to the forehead, the belly, then to the right and then left shoulder before a half bow. We lean forward to kiss icons glittering with a gemstone halo. Candles flicker everywhere, the crowd around me adding to them endlessly.

We pause to sing *a cappella.* I mouth the words as if knowing the unfamiliar chants and songs. An elaborately attired priest in gold vestments shakes silver censors of incense. He then leads a series of additional chants. The churchgoers listen carefully, crossing themselves and bowing at apparently the right moments.

I'm too enthralled with the cathedral to even try to understand what is going on around me. The place is enormous and lavish, its stained glass competing with a series of concentric arches covered with paintings that reach so high they might be headed for heaven. Gilded bas-reliefs and paintings of Christ and the apostles cover the interior. Jewels and precious stones glisten from floor to the highest dome. Crowds mingle and move from icon to icon, from iconostasis to paintings. No one stands still for long. The almost overpowering scent of incense, and warmth, and the flicker of hundreds of candles add to the sense of spirituality.

I don't know how to pray, but I try. Positioning myself in front of one of the icons of the Virgin Mother and the baby Jesus, I light one of the candles mother has handed me. I stand there for several minutes, repeating silent prayers, asking God to protect my new family—and myself.

⌬⌬⌬

One afternoon we go to tea at someone else's house, which, more than our own home, resembles a true palace. We are only a short walk away, so Mother has deemed it safe to take her precious daughters that far.

It is snowing, as usual. We dodge white piles higher than our carport in Dallas. Bundled in furs and muffs, Larissa and I chatter happily, both resisting the urge to pelt one another with snowballs. On the streets, the mood seems more buoyant than usual. Smiles appear on faces that usually seem angry or depressed. More than a few people stop to embrace one another joyfully. Is it a holiday of some kind?

We bring calling cards ourselves this time, and are escorted into an elaborate room with an organ, divan, fancy chairs that appear too fragile for sitting, plush carpets woven with animal scenes, and walls hung with gorgeous paintings of scenery and royal portraits. Our hostess, Countess Maria Ivanovna Shoblonsky, greets us enthusiastically.

"Have you heard the news?" she blurts out while pouring tea. "He's dead!"

"Who?" my mother and sister ask at once.

"The Mad Monk. Father Grigory. Murdered, they say."

I am probably the only one in the room of richly attired ladies who expresses no surprise at Rasputin's death.

The noise level, however, definitely rises to a frenzy of gossip and speculation. Some of the ladies dab their eyes with embroidered handkerchiefs, while others look scandalized. My mother is one of the few who express relief.

I attack the bread and fruit preserves while speculation swirls around me.

"They say the empress has taken to her bed in grief. She must be heart-broken."

"This will change everything, don't you think? Everyone has wanted him gone from her boudoir for years."

"Oh, I don't believe all that nonsense. He was her spiritual adviser, nothing more."

"But the newspapers—"

"The newspapers will say anything. The tsar gives them way too much freedom."

"Did you hear that he refused to die?"

"I hear he was poisoned."

"No, no, he was shot multiple times."

"I have it on good authority that they dragged him out of the Malaya Nevka. He drowned right near the Moika Palace."

I know the Little Neva River from our limited carriage rides, and since I spend all my free time staring out my bedroom window at another canal, can well imagine the scene.

"Pushed in, most likely."

"They say Yusupov did it," one lady whispers.

"Do you mean the Prince? Surely not."

"Well, the corpse was found—"

"So you think it was Yusupov?"

"Who else? He and the Grand Duke, according to my chamber maid."

"But I just saw Father Grigory two days ago. He helped me tremendously," one of the women dressed all in black murmurs, tears smearing her thick make-up.

"Now, Baroness, you know he was not a real holy man," another chides.

"When will the funeral be?" our hostess asks. "Surely it will be quite the event."

"They say…well, they say there will not be one. The body cannot be seen yet, but an autopsy is being performed even as we speak."

"So are we sure it is him?"

"Quite. His daughters identified his boots yesterday, and now the body has been inspected."

One woman crosses herself. "God rest his soul—"

"You mean God Rest Russia. He was a threat to everything," another interrupts. "He had the tsaritsa enthralled to the point she could not think straight. And no doubt he *was* a German spy."

"There will be no better way for us to begin the new year." my mother chimes in then, crossing herself, as well. "Perhaps the tsar will return from the front and straighten out the government."

I've already figured out that while, here it is mid-December, in the rest of the world they use a different calendar, in which the dates are ahead of Russia's by almost two weeks. Plus, everyone keeps mentioning January seventh will be Christmas, rather than December twenty-fifth.

Not that you can tell we are approaching a holiday by looking around this palace or our own home. Apparently, not only are Christmas trees forbidden due to their German origins, but imported greenery and decorations are unavailable or prohibited. Or perhaps people are burning them for heat, the way we hear that some of the peasants have done with their furniture.

"I do so miss our fir tree," Larissa complains about once a day.

"Be quiet," I told her yesterday. "At least Mother and apparently everyone else has forgotten about any kind of the usual fasting."

"True." She glanced at me then, somewhat mischievously, and I could almost predict what would come next. "Some of us could stand to lose a bit of weight."

I tossed some silver tinsel in her hair. We had found it in a box at the back of a closet, along with a strand of lights we'd just wound around the bannister of the grand staircase.

"*I'm* not the one who eats a half dozen pastries at tea," I reminded her, but smiling.

Forgetting our respective ages, we chased each other for a while, taking turns draping each other's clothing with tinsel before collapsing in laughter just before Mother entered the parlor and admired our festive lights.

Now, looking around at the elaborate décor, I notice for the first time that the countess has no decorations whatsoever in her receiving room. Perhaps Larissa and I should have refrained from trying to make it seem like a holiday in such sober times. Yet it had made all of us happy for at least a short time. I even heard a servant softly humming a Christmas carol this morning.

We stay much longer than appropriate in high society, as do the others. Everyone seems unwilling to miss out on any of the juiciest gossip. But at last we say our good-byes and trudge back home, and this time I realize the reason for all the smiles on the narrow streets.

The next day we learn that there is, indeed, to be no public funeral for Rasputin. From the efficient communication system provided by almost daily teas, we also hear that the tsaritsa and her daughters have already held a private imperial service for him on the grounds of their palace. No one knows exactly where he is buried, although other rumor-mongers claim a chapel is being built on the site. Most of the tea ladies, as I now refer to them mentally, seem outraged at this piece of news, as it certainly deprives them of the scandalous stories a regular funeral might have provided.

Even I am disappointed. If I am trapped in history, it seems only fair that I should get to see some famous people from the period—even the dead ones.

Chapter 6

L arissa is to be married. He is an officer in the same regiment as our father, and a match apparently ecstatically welcomed by our parents. Exactly how and when this all came about I have not asked, since I'm still somewhat wary about betraying my ignorance. I cannot help wondering every day: *if I am here, then where is the real Olga?* Trapped at Grandma Olga's house with Cheryl? But she cannot be, of course, because in my time she has already died. Unless she is Julie, and now figuring out how she became a teenager living with her own granddaughter.

And what if I do something that changes the future? That, admittedly, is rapidly becoming my biggest fear. I've seen enough television shows and films in which people somehow get transported via a machine into the past, and one bit of interference changes the entire future. In the movies, this kind of interference can mean some-one—like myself—never gets born! What happens if I get Olga's body—or my/our body—damaged or even killed?

Silent screams continue to haunt my nights.

Since I have neither a rational way to explain my predicament to my family here nor do I want to alarm them about the possible fate of the genuine Olga, I have decided for now to listen more and speak less.

Fortunately, everyone around me spends hours talking: about the war, the potential fate of the monarchy, the revolutionaries, and which government official is the most corrupt. Even with Rasputin gone, his and the tsarit-sa's succession of misplaced ministerial appointments live on.

Father sends us regular telegrams, but it's obvious he chooses his words carefully. He gives no hint when he will come home again, and, in spite of myself, I find I share my mother and sister's worry for his safety—and for that of my future brother-in-law, whose name is Pavel.

The tea ladies continue to keep us well informed, and store windows post telegrams with war news. They also post endless lists of the dead. More and more ladies show up in the afternoon wearing black mourning dresses or black armbands.

I've become not only an excellent seamstress and knitter, but a killer at dominoes, which I much prefer to the other games Larissa favors. I suspect she is getting sick of losing to me, but if she weren't so busy chatting about her precious Pavel's golden hair and handsome physique, she might have a chance to win occasionally.

But Larissa or Lara, as we call her often, is not a fluff-head. Each day I watch her in her room writing letters or praying at her icons in a red corner. The miniature frames filled with layers of paint remind me of Grandma Olga's icons. When I ask about them, Larissa gives me an odd look but patiently points each out: Saint Serafim, Saint Anna of Novgorod, and the Virgin Mary. Her favorite is the latter, its frame surrounded by silver filigree and the blue-gowned mother and child haloed in gold leaf.

Saint Anna is encrusted with actual tiny jewels, although I prefer the one of Saint Serafim, whoever he is or was. With his long white hair and matching beard, he could pass for Santa Claus or the Russian St. Nicholas if he didn't appear so gaunt and wear a waist-length copper crucifix. He perches on a rock, one hand upraised toward heaven, and the other reaching out to a bear that appears to be eating out of his hand. In the background, a forest of birch trees frames the scene just as a gold halo rims his head.

Admittedly, the icons are stunning, especially the one of Saint Anna. However, no matter how much time I spend here, I cannot grasp the total significance of the painted spiritual frames. I can only admire the time she spends praying and crossing herself in the corner. Sometimes she presses her lips and then forehead to them, the way I've seen people do in the cathedral, but I have no idea why.

ϾᴼϾᴼ

My mother accompanies us the day we make a trip to a nearby hospital that appears to be twenty times the size of the first one. She wants to check out conditions for herself, and also to deliver scarves she has knitted for the soldiers.

Although not grandiose and sumptuous, this palace-turned-hospital still manages to juxtapose beauty with suffering and poverty in a way that depresses me as much as the soldiers themselves do. It is obvious that tapestries and mirrors once covered the walls. In what must've once functioned as a ballroom, tightly packed rows of beds stretch for what seems like half the length of a football field.

Now, chaos reigns.

The soldiers in one of beds I approach at mid-morning just stares at me. "Are you one of them?" he finally asks as I offer him water.

"One of what?"

"One of the elite. The damned *bourgeoisie*!"

"I'm—no, I'm just a nurse. Or a nurse's aide, I suppose."

"I don't believe you. You'll go home to your huge home and forget you were ever here. I hear that even the German bitch takes care of soldiers. As if that makes up for everything." Before I realize it, he has spit his water back out at me. "Go home, witch!"

I hurry past him and skip two beds. I'm shaking with something like fear, but am also angry. After all, I know that he is right, but it doesn't seem fair to hate me for being who I am. Or having what I have.

Moving from bed to bed, I manage to forget about the spitting mad soldier, and concentrate on those who seem grateful for any care or attention. Some even look at me admiringly, and others ask about my family. "I have a sister here, too," I tell them. "And my father is at the front with the tsar."

After a while, I omit the last three words. Any mention of the tsar changes grins to frowns.

A few men have severe burns. "Damn mustard gas," one man explains as I change his dressing, and then he breaks into tears.

"I did it myself," another soldier whispers to me, pointing to where his feet used to be. "I borrowed someone's gun and just shot them off one day and started crawling home. It was my Christmas gift to myself."

He attempts a smile. I attempt not to judge. I've already caught several soldiers picking at their stitches, as if removing them will prolong their stay in a place with heat and food.

There isn't one soul in Petrograd who does not know we are losing the war and that the soldiers are leaving the front by the thousands—without permission, but without being stopped. I wonder what the officers think, and how helpless they must feel. Again and again, soldiers tell me stories that are hard to hear—of missing weapons and supplies, of absent medics or long waits for medical attention, of starvation so serious they were forced to eat the horses' food, of frostbite, of poison gasses, of mass desertions.

One soldier admits to me that he would have killed himself if only he could have found a bullet.

Most of the men are thinly clad, unlike at the well-funded Feodorovsky Gorodok. I notice even those with all their limbs often have no boots or shoes under their cots. Instead, they wrap their feet in pieces of cloth, paper, or whatever they have been able to find.

I am so busy focusing on feet I fail to notice what is happening two beds down my row. A doctor stands beside the bed flanked by two nurses and wielding what appears to be a saw. Before my mind registers the implications of this, the doctor begins to hack away at the patient's leg. In spite of the nurses' best efforts to control the situation, blood spurts everywhere and the soldier screams. I have heard echoes of such screams all day, but they always seemed far away in another hall. Apparently, the doctor has moved to my area since the surgical ward is overcrowded.

Unwilling to watch any more, I turn and hurry up the rows of cots, heading for an exit to the palace grounds. On the outdoor staircase, I throw up last night's pastries and appetizers. When I'm done, I dry heave for several more minutes, crying almost simultaneously.

I will not go back in there. I will not watch someone hack off limbs. No dream—or nightmare—should include so much gruesome reality. If this is not a dream, I want out. Out of this place where, based on the number of bodies someone is casually dumping into a truck in front of me, people do not survive. Or, based on what I saw inside, wish they had not.

For a long time I watch the truck with its load of bodies pull away and get replaced by another empty truck. I will not, I keep saying to myself. *I will not.* Eventually this is where Larissa and my mother find me, at roughly the same time as a toot of the horn announces Mikhail's arrival.

"Thank God the car is running," Larissa says. Then, apparently noting the blood and fluids covering my apron and sleeves, she chides, "You should've washed up. And we've looked everywhere for you. Are you okay?"

I can only nod, sinking gratefully into the huge back seat. As if sensing my horror and mental exhaustion, Larissa and my mother chat with one another. I just want to go *home*!

ભૹભ

The holidays pass quietly and quickly, almost as if we never moved from 1916 to 1917. We do, however, spend Christmas Eve at church, one of the few nights the streets are quieter than usual, but so crowded with starving faces and shivering soldiers that I can only pick at the plates full of food—complete with a Christmas goose— the servants carry to our table the next day.

Still, I'm grateful to be in a wealthy family, even though the idea of what the future—the very near future, from what I'm hearing as the protests get larger and noisier—scares me. I try to convince my mother to ask the servants to cut back on the food and to store some of it, but she pays little attention.

Just when I've decided to put some pressure on Monsieur Bordet, he suddenly stops coming. We've heard nothing from him, and one of the tea ladies says it's quite normal for such things to happen.

"Not everyone is loyal," she murmurs, and then adds more loudly as she reaches for a scone, "and people do seem to disappear for no reason these days."

All this misery is immediately forgotten one day in February when an invitation to the Alexander Palace arrives. Although balls have been canceled for the duration of the war, apparently parties and a limited number of gala events have not. This one is supposed to be a state dinner in honor of some British diplomats, and even though I am only seventeen—or so they tell me now--and Larissa nineteen, we are both to be permitted once again to attend. It appears our family is being invited because my mother's family is from the British nobility, something I also just learned.

While I am being dressed by Tanya, I try to get her to talk to me, although for months she has remained reticent. "Do you like your job?" I ask, realizing at the same time that it is an unfair question. Who, if given a choice, would opt to wait on rich people's every whim? Larissa once told me that over a thousand servants work at the Alexander Palace in Tsarskoe Selo—to take care of just seven family members.

Tanya does not answer at first. "It is a good position," she states finally, and I wonder if the poke in my back when she laces my corset is accidental. "I provide for my family as well as I can."

"That must be difficult with all the rationing and shortages."

"That is why I like my job. Food to eat and a warm place to stay all day." She says the words softly, and I murmur something sympathetic, but really have no idea how to react. We might as well be separated by miles instead of inches, since we move in two disparate societies.

Tonight my gown swirls around me in a ruffled effect of lavender satin. The material is heavy enough for the weather, but I fear I may have heat stroke once we go inside. Perhaps the palace will be subject to fuel rationing, as well. I consider wearing the amber beads, but they definitely do not match. Still, I have been wearing them almost daily, even hidden beneath my necklines, because for some reason I know they must be the key to my return to the future. So far, they have not seemed to do anything except stay warm to the touch, but I now know that all amber is that way.

Still, the plunging neckline of my dress demands something showy, and Tanya brings me a diamond and amethyst pendant. I am dazzled by its beauty, as well as my own reflection in the mirror, although I have no idea how to maneuver through the evening wearing elbow-length white gloves.

Tanya has pinned my auburn hair up in curls, and I look sophisticated and even gorgeous, I think immodestly, twirling around in front of the floor-length mirror. The pendant probably cost enough to feed at least two dozen families, but it is a thought I push away. It's not my fault I'm rich, after all. I was born into it—or fell into it, as I think of my presence in the early twentieth century.

No sled tonight, as the car seems to be running again and it is snowing dreadfully. Plus, as I recall, the Alexander Palace is miles away. I worry about the strikers blocking the roads and throwing snowballs at our chauffeured car. However, all is quieter than usual on Nevsky Prospekt, with the exception of rows of cars and carriages unloading people dressed in finery at brightly lit restaurants and theaters. Then I chide myself for being judgmental. Here *I* am en route to an elegant party, for god's sake.

This time I walk in confidently, sure of my social—and language—skills, as well as court etiquette. We are escorted through several rooms to a long table in a sumptuous dining room illuminated by chandeliers and heated by a series of lit stoves. Everywhere I look, out-of-season flowers bloom in towering vases—lavish bouquets of hyacinths, mimosa, irises, and lilacs. Yet the cloying scent of competing perfumes and colognes overwhelms them, and I worry about sneezing into my food.

It is surprising to see the tsar again, as I would have expected him to be at the war front or in the Winter Palace in Petrograd dealing with all the unrest. His face appears thinner and hollower than two months ago, and his smiles never seem to reach those brilliant blue eyes.

By contrast, the tsaritsa's eyes, the color of pale marbles, seem as cold as the diamonds glittering on her wrists and in her reddish-gold hair, which is powdered with gray. She looks half sad, half angry, although elegant in a cream silk gown embroidered in blue and silver. A heavy scent of roses swirls around her. I am fascinated by this empress whose actions and behavior have and will contribute so heavily to her monarchy's downfall, and a tiny shiver runs through me whenever I look at her and the sapphire cross dangling from her neck.

Everyone speaks English this evening, unlike the French at the last event, and we are seated at one of the many tables set for thirteen. The emperor visits our table once, and I can barely keep from staring. It is still difficult to be here, knowing what will happen. Knowing that outside and across Russia his people are starving—and planning a revolution. Knowing that I may be stuck in the middle of it at any time. Knowing that this man, the entire imperial family, and many of the dinner guests will be dead very soon.

The dinner conversation, which seems to last forever and requires a lot of waltzing around subject matter, would be excruciating were it not for the endless procession of superb dishes served. We feast happily on cream of barley soup, veal, chicken, trout, cucumber salad and, for dessert, a sort of tangerine ice. No shortages here, unless the royal family splurged to impress the British who apparently are also at war.

The glitter of electric chandeliers, the porcelain stoves, and the dizzying array of diamonds, sapphires, and emeralds adorning women's hair, necks, wrists, and even shoulders eventually begin to give me a headache. Two ladies near me flash their jewels incessantly, like out-of-control mating fireflies. They are talking about a dinner they attended the previous night and laughing about how someone poured champagne over someone else's head.

Surprisingly, a gentleman in uniform leans across the table and scolds them: "My dear ladies, are you aware that at one hundred rubles per bottle, champagne costs

roughly five or six times what the average Russian worker earns?"

They flash their wrist diamonds again, as if flicking
away a bug, and one of them tells him primly, "This is
the tsar's night. We don't need to ruin it talking politics."

The gentleman stands up and politely nods to us
while announcing he is heading for the billiards room.
Perhaps he knows what I suspect: that this is quite likely
the last state dinner the Romanov family will ever give.

Chapter 7

One pale, late winter afternoon, I'm reading some of Pushkin's verses when the noise along the canal reaches a crescendo of shouts and cheers. Leaning out my bedroom window, I observe people embracing even more exuberantly than they did when Rasputin was murdered.

I run downstairs to see Larissa and my mother both peering out the parlor windows. "What is happening? Is the war over?" I ask, doubting that this is true, but I cannot remember how and when it ended in Russia.

"We don't know," my mother—whose full name I now know is Anna Petrovna Sheretno—replies.

"Perhaps something has happened to the tsar," Larissa adds, crossing herself.

"May I go out and see?" I suggest, although knowing how protective she is of both Larissa and myself, I have little hope of my request being granted.

She predictably refuses to entertain the possibility.

Upstairs, I reach under the mattress to where I have secreted a stolen dress and a head scarf I found downstairs in the maids' quarters. It had been hanging there for weeks, and I knew the day would come when I would want to go out and explore on my own. The only possibility—at least the only safe one—seems to be to do this dressed as a servant, since I notice that except for squabbling over food outside the shops, no one except the police actually hurls things at the poor people or the soldiers.

Fortunately, the house has several entrances, including one at the back for servants. If anyone has seen me, I cannot tell, but within minutes of changing, I'm alongside the canal and strolling briskly toward Nevsky Prospekt.

I catch snatches of conversation as people pass, but it is not until reaching the Nevsky that I realize some of what is happening. Literally thousands of women crowd the avenue, a few holding signs: *Down With the War* and *Down With the Autocracy*. Most, however, chant in unison, *davaite nam khleb*, over, and over: give us bread.

I don't see any of the tsar's soldiers or police, but note that many women carry sticks, pieces of cobblestone, and large ice chunks.

While attempting to pause and take it all in, I'm

swept away like the middle fish in a giant school of minnows. There is no place to go but forward, wedged between thousands of people marching along Nevsky Prospekt.

Soon I recognize the enormous columns of Kazan Cathedral, where Mother took us to church once. Today the crowds camped out between its circular wings seem embraced by another power, and no one is begging God for bread. Instead, they beg the tsar *in absentia*. Or the government. I am not sure who is in charge. Petrograd seems to be alive with its own sense of destiny.

I should be afraid. After all, although incognito, I am one of those who has plenty of fresh bread daily and butter most of the time. Feeling somewhat guilty and reluctant to stand out in this determined crowd, I raise my voice with the other women: *davaite nam khleb!*

From windows of buildings, more women wave and cheer. From side streets and canals, groups of men, both soldiers and workers, emerge to swell our ranks. We become a gigantic brigade moving more and more slowly as the crowd widens, banners sometimes falling and slapping some poor unsuspecting soul in the face.

Signs representing specific groups, from striking metalworkers to textile factories, add an incongruous splash of color to the otherwise drab clothing of the marching poor.

Everywhere people shove leaflets in our hands, until Nevsky Prospekt is paved with a kaleidoscopic litter of colors and words insisting *Our Children Are Starving* or urging people to join various political parties.

I find myself caught up in the mayhem, unworried even about how to get home. I am part of something large today—what I have learned from all the signs is International Women's Day—and long to see what will happen next.

Sometimes it gets dangerous. Small children, their voices barely heard in the crowds, call out for bread and herring, nearly tripping us as they race anxiously in and out of what has become an ever-moving labyrinth of adults.

Occasionally a group pauses and heaves a chunk of ice at a store window, causing contingents of marchers to rush inside and attempt to loot the nearly empty shelves. People emerge clutching their prizes, from a few potatoes to dishes and clothing.

Scarlet trams park in the middle of the avenue, stalled by the crowds and unable to proceed. Most shops and businesses have put up *closed* signs, their owners either fearful for their lives and their merchandise, or out of sympathy for the various causes being touted.

A policeman does appear sporadically, but always standing and watching, making no move to interfere. I don't know if it is because the police are sympathetic or afraid. They are certainly outnumbered about a thousand to one, so either possibility seems likely.

Eventually I yearn to make personal contact with

some of the women pressed almost against me now, but everyone keeps chanting or yelling. My one attempt— "Isn't this exciting?"—must have been the wrong approach, as the *babushka* gives me the critical look that old Russian women have perfected, turns away, and continues chanting.

Perhaps "exciting" *is* the wrong word. Even absurd, considering the stark poverty these people live with.

Belatedly, I recall rumors of typhus among the homeless, but am too close to too many people to protect myself from the illness. Besides, I haven't picked it up from my hospital work, and I attempt to shrug the worry away.

I admit to myself that until now I've been a somewhat dispassionate observer of an entire city or nation's desperate resolve. Even today, I can fight my way back through the crowds at any time and sit down in my warm parlor for tea and pastries. I don't suffer from lack of bread, job security, or even wages. But if I did, I feel confident I'd be marching with these people as a "real" protester. I've seen the way the nobility live, and the gap is so disproportionate that the government is bound to fall.

Most of the women have now linked arms, and we march as endless, unbreakable human chains down the avenue.

At one point, just after passing the Gostiny Dvor shopping center with its empty shelves, I catch a glimpse of a monument to Catherine the Great. Her unmistakable likeness seems to overlook the marching placidly. What would she think of all this? I smile, deciding that under the great empress, things would never have regressed so far. After all, she ruled Russia during both the American and French revolutions, and still managed to keep her empire an intact monarchy.

It occurs to me, as Catherine the Second passes out of view, how unusual it is to see a monument anywhere. From what I've gleaned from Larissa and others, many of them have been dismantled and moved elsewhere to protect them from bombs, or sheathed with cloth to hide them.

I debate turning around. If we continue to move eastward, the crowd will end up making the trek all the way to Alexander Nevsky Cathedral and the cemeteries where most the great Russian writers and composers are buried. It is a long walk in the bitter cold, with only the giant snow piles seeming to reach out like a mother's embrace to warm the street.

My mother and Larissa, who have surely missed me by now, would be shocked to know where I am and must be worried sick.

Besides, my back and feet are killing me.

Anxiously now, I unlock arms from the women on both sides of me and weave to the left, where a new group of protesters has changed direction and suddenly headed west, perhaps intent on reaching the Winter Palace. I decide I'd better join them.

It takes a while to maneuver sideways through a crowd that moves like a series of human tanks, but at last I am in the midst of the swelling westward marchers.

By now, I am shivering in the subzero temperatures, and the warmth of bodies provides as much comfort as a sense of solidarity.

As I suspected, this group seems more intent on criticizing the government than demanding bread. The placards and banners, ranging from *Down With the Tsar* to obscenities about the empress, are more angry than desperate.

Many of these marchers appear to be coal workers—or unemployed ones, since I've heard the factories are closed for lack of coal, this time due to a railroad blockade.

Other lines of women stand patiently for the length of the avenue in some kind of a line that might be for bread. Or eggs. Or butter. Or sugar. These people, most of whom appear gaunt and weary as they patiently endure the snowflakes drifting to the ground, seem to spend their entire day trying to acquire the necessities of life. It would be a wonder if anyone were working at all.

A small contingent of soldiers plays musical instruments and sings songs I don't know. Someone steps in front of me and shoves a sign at my gloveless hand, and soon I find myself waving *Give Power to the Soviet*.

By the time we've moved almost to Palace Square and the opportunity to duck down a side street closer to home, I have been nearly beheaded by the banners of at least two fellow marchers.

Hurrying through the increasingly larger flow of people flooding the city, I have no idea how I will slip unnoticed inside my house, nor how I will account for my absence or my working class attire.

Fortunately, the servants' entrance is unlocked, and I slide in quietly.

Just before reaching my bedroom, I nearly run into one of the servants sweeping the hall floor. I put my head down and hurry inside my room where I can wash up and change clothes.

She sees me, but doesn't see me. That's the life she has always led, I suspect, and, presumably, the same philosophy that the nobility to which I belong also views the world: we look, but we do not see.

Chapter 8

Days pass even more slowly now that I've seen some of what is happening in the city. Apparently, I have gotten away with my secret excursion, and also notice myself becoming much more defensive about the revolutionaries. My mother and I cannot help hearing rifle shots from the street and on nearby rooftops, where police and soldiers return gunfire from the mobs.

The protests themselves seem louder and more desperate as each day progresses.

Helpless to do anything, we instead argue constantly about the future, and I cannot always find ways to back up what I know without revealing how I obtained my information.

Mother is a beautiful woman, whose eyes become flashing emeralds when she is angry with me, which seems to happen daily.

"We should make a plan to evacuate," I insist. "We may be forced to leave our home and not have time to pack anything."

"I've told you, no one is going anywhere! The monarchy is under pressure, but we have survived before. Don't forget about 1905." She's referring to Bloody Sunday, the day the tsar's troops fired on peaceful crowds who'd marched to the Winter Palace demanding bread. I say a silent prayer of thanks to my history teacher and to Olga for the books she sent for my project and sometimes with the Christmas sweaters.

"Mother, this has gone way beyond that revolution. This involves the entire country. Soon there will be no tsar, no nobility, and no palaces for individual families. They will just take them, like they did our automobile!"

Yesterday, our chauffeur was overtaken by crowds near one of the canals and forced to get out and walk while several men confiscated our car. Mikhail is still shaken and cannot stop blaming himself.

The horses disappeared days ago. I'd rather not know what happened to them.

"No tsar? Are you truly mad, Olga?" Larissa joins the fight. Her own tourmaline eyes open wide in shock. "I don't care what the rumors say, it's just not possible. The Romanovs have ruled Russia for over three hundred years, and, God willing, they will rule at least another three hundred."

She crosses herself and starts muttering, and I resist the urge to reach over and interrupt her fingers in mid cross. I have begun to feel something like love for my sister, too, but she can be entirely too innocent—and too pious—for my own disposition.

I try again. "Other countries survive fine without tsars or kings. Look what happened in America! But to get to that point—well, let's not forget the heads that rolled in France."

This time my sister and mother synchronize as they cross themselves. "*Bozhe moi*. My God!" she storms. "How dare you even bring up such a thing? It's sacrilegious to speak about monarchs getting murdered."

But they will be, I long to say, biting the inside of my cheek to keep the words in check. I, too, in spite of only a few glimpses and hasty formal introductions to what appeared to be a lovely imperial family, do not want to think of the executions I know will come.

"Just consider packing, at least," I say more calmly and retreat to my room.

Up here, I can at least be alone with my worries. Often I read Pushkin's stories and poems, or short stories by Nikolai Gogol. I especially enjoy the latter, since Gogol sets his stories in a surreal Petersburg that reminds me of my own situation. In one story, a man chases his own life-size, uniformed nose all over the city. No one seems to notice how discombobulated events are, yet they occur in a far more peaceful, whimsical Petrograd/Petersburg. And after all, it is no odder to awaken and find someone else's nose in a loaf of your breakfast bread than to awaken and find yourself living in that same strange city more than seven decades before you were born.

Sometimes I want to just scream and scream.

೮⌀೮⌀

At tea time several days after sneaking out and joining the protesters, I come downstairs. Yet again, I am reminded of Wonderland. You would think that with a revolution going on outside and the government all but collapsed, these women would have something better to do than slather butter—"It's the best butter, you know"—on their bread, but if anything the three-to-five crowd has thickened with tea ladies.

By now, it truly does feel as if I am at the Mock Turtle's table, where it is tea time all the time, and where the guests all huddle together at one side of the parlor. To complicate matters, conversations go on in some combination of three languages: French, English, and Russian.

Today is unusually noisy. Every other sentence begins *govoryat*. They say: "They say the tsar has given up the throne."

"Nikolai Aleksandrovitch, abdicate? *Neelsya*. Not possible. He would never—"

"So will Tsar Alexei succeed him?"

"They say—" One of the women leans over and dips her hat feather into her tea. "—that the heir is not healthy enough to rule."

"They say Kerensky is in charge. That there will not be a monarchy anymore."

"*Neelsya*. This nation cannot operate without a tsar."

"But it hasn't been operating at all for a long time," I suggest hesitantly.

Everyone disregards me.

"*Govoryat* we will have a government like France. Or perhaps America."

"But it would never work here. Our peasants cannot support themselves without help, let alone run a country on their own. Just look at the problems the Duma has had governing, and they are mainly aristocratic politicians."

"We need more time," Larissa chimes in bravely. "Time for the tsar to sort out all these riots and protests and shootings."

"I'm afraid we're out of time," a countess says firmly.

"It's all a riddle to me," someone else joins in. "Everything was going so well until this dreadful war."

Another woman turns to her. "Are you saying the war caused the revolution or that the revolution is causing us to lose the war—"

"I blame the weather," someone else interrupts. "My husband says that not only has the blockade forced the trains to take a longer route, but the tracks are drifted with snow and many of the boilers are freezing and bursting."

"Of course, the countess is correct. Were it not for the war, our soldiers could get back to their farms and produce more food."

"Not to mention other necessities. Have you seen the price of soap? My maid says it costs nearly six times what it did. And with my delicate skin…"

As interested as I am, the conversation never seems to go anywhere new. No one takes the blame for anything, and no one seems willing to concede anything, let alone acknowledge the frozen bodies increasingly littering the main roads. It's as if we're here for a bit of revolutionary gossip, but everyone fails to attempt to explore what it all means or what will happen beyond the following week.

I resist checking my watch. An elderly woman has nodded off. I reach over and carefully set her tea cup on a table before it falls. A servant quickly removes it and circles the room serving more milk and sugar, and I wonder what she must be thinking about all this. Normally, my mother does some of the tea serving herself, but today's crowd is too large for her to handle.

I try to cool my temper and resist interfering to the point of rudeness by playing mind games. My brain leaves the tea party while I play one I like when I'm trying to kill time.

I word associate, starting with a particular letter: fancy, feather, fruit, flowers, farce, ferret, fellow, fortune, freak, failure, forget, future—

"*Govoryat*—" A voice interrupts me at the word I don't want to consider. "—that the empress may be arrested."

"Never. *Neelzya.*"

"But she really is that hated by the people."

"How can the Russian people hate their little father and little mother? Did you see her at the hospitals in that Red Cross uniform?"

"*Govoryat* all the children are ill, but no one knows if it is true."

"Well, I have it on very good sources that it *is* true. They have the measles."

"Ah, well, then they cannot be so cruel as to arrest her. And then what? Will there be a trial?"

"Darling, is there any more of that wonderful mint tea left?"

"Yes, do pour me some more, as well." The lady with the wet feather has a tiny drip leaking down the brim of her hat.

The conversation turns to which ministers might be retained and which promoted or exiled to Siberia, and I sneak quietly out of the room—protocol or no protocol. I have to find a way to get out of more than just this room.

Like Alice, I have apparently fallen down some kind of hole, and I *must* get out of this unusual, horrid place.

ఁఎఁ

As days go by, we learn many of the rumors are true. A man named Kerensky is in charge of the new provisional government—although a separate group of councils called the Soviets rule, too—the imperial children still have the measles, and the Romanov family is under house arrest at Alexander Palace. We even had a new tsar for about one day: Nicholas II's brother Mikhail, who apparently had the good sense to abdicate before he took over.

From home, we can smell smoke as ministry buildings and police stations burn.

The soldiers and revolutionaries have coalesced into one band, and none of us dares go outside anymore. Across the river, thousands of prisoners have been released from the Peter and Paul Fortress to join that pandemonium.

Most of our servants fail to show up for work, although we have no idea if they cannot get here or choose not to do so.

We hear less news than usual, as at last the tea parties and the tea invitations cease.

In the midst of all the uncertainty, someone pounds on the front door.

Terrified of opening it, I'm surprised when Larissa responds to the voice yelling outside and races to unlock it. From the tearful embraces they exchange, I assume this must be the golden-haired Pavel Pavlovich Mebedsov.

Larissa's fiancé does not look much different than any other soldier, and just as disheveled. His rifle has a red flag tied to it, and when he hugs us and sees me looking at it, "It's the only way I can get through the city without getting shot by my own men," he explains. "Or anyone, for that matter. Any officers or soldiers who have remained loyal to the Old Guard have been removed or killed."

Mother gasps but quickly recovers and brings him a blanket and a cup of tea. Larissa sits close to him on the divan, her melted gemlike eyes never leaving his face.

He *is* handsome, in spite of all the scratches on his cheeks. But most of the time, he covers his face with his hands as he tries to tell us some of what he has lived through and witnessed. "At Kronstadt they killed the officers," he says quietly. "Just buried them all—living and dead—side by side.

"There are armored cars everywhere, smashing and burning palaces and government buildings," he continues, voice trembling. "When the firemen arrive, they are chased away because the crowds want to see things burn."

"Is there any word of Sergei? Have you seen my husband?" My mother forces a brave tone that fools no one.

"I'm sorry, Anna Petrovna, I haven't seen him in

days. And you haven't heard from him, either? Not even a telegram?"

Mother shakes her head and then, her resolve broken, starts to cry. I bring her a cup of tea and a biscuit, pausing to stroke the hair that resembles mine.

Telegrams no longer send lists of the dead or injured, and the military has apparently dissolved into chaos. After what Lieutenant Mebedsov has told us, we dare not speculate about Father's fate, but can only hope the next knock on the door is his.

"Lara, I'm here to take you away with me. Olga and your mother, too, if they will come. I've seen what the mobs have done to some of the mansions, and it's too dangerous to stay in the city."

"But my darling, it is almost Holy Week! We cannot possibly leave right now—"

"Lara," Mother interrupts. "We've had this conversation about *Pascha*, and you know we cannot—"

"Cannot make *pashka* or *kulich*, I know," Lara says fiercely. "I understand we will not be able to find the raisins or butter or almonds for those, let alone roast pork. And maybe we cannot take confession or maybe not even *attend* mass, but we can still stay here and make and do something to honor our Lord's resurrection!"

"Olga and I can do that without you if we have to, my dear daughter."

"But I already have the willow twigs for Palm Sunday. And I've hidden away a smidgen of vanilla and even traded some of my lace for some dried fruits and you know I'm *always* the one who dyes the eggs!"

"My mother will want you to help," the lieutenant reassures her. "We still have much more of such things in the countryside. Soon our gardens will produce all that we need to eat. And," he adds, glancing almost shyly yet worriedly at his betrothed's figure, "it is obvious that you've done more than enough fasting in preparation for the holiday. Your life, my sweet one—that is what God would want you to preserve, not vanilla and fruits."

Then, returning his attention to us, he tries again. "We have plenty of space in the country, and I can assure your safety—at least more than you have here. Please, Olga Sergeievna and Anna Petrovna. Accompany us."

As my mother continues to protest, he tells us more stories. "The Kschessinska mansion is no more, at least in any livable form. The crowds have gutted it, smashed the great ballerina's grand piano into splinters, poured ink on the carpets, even destroyed the bathtubs and filled them with cigarette butts. You're much safer at my family's country home way outside Tsarskoe Selo."

"No, my dear son," my mother insists, her tears now dried. "You may take Lara away to be safe—and Olga if she wants to go—but I will not leave my home until or unless I hear from my husband."

"But isn't Tsarskoe Selo occupied by troops now because the tsar's family is there?" I ask, without revealing my true objection to leaving. Somehow, this place is connected to my arrival in the past, and I cling to the belief that it holds the key to getting me back to my own time. Yet I want my mother and sister to be safe, and in spite of the presence of the tsar and his family in Tsarskoye Selo, it surely must be safer for them there than staying in the capital.

My sister begs us both to change our minds, but she is no match for our collaborative stubbornness. At last, she agrees to gather some clothes and belongings.

"Lara." Pavel catches her by the hand. "Bring only your warmest but least elegant gowns. We do not know what the future holds, and to appear as a part of the nobility is too dangerous. Dress simply. Borrow a servant's outfit if you must."

Larissa heads reluctantly upstairs to pack, but I get the feeling she will come back down and refuse at the last minute.

While Pavel cleans up, Mother finds him some of the simpler, non-military wear of my father's. They are about the same height and weight, and before either of us can raise an eyebrow, he has torn a few seams, walked over to the fireplace, and rubbed some of the ashes on his new shirt and coat.

He pulls me aside. "It is even worse than I told your sister and mother," he whispers. "Not long ago one of the admirals was grabbed, stripped, and made to stand on the ice. They lit him on fire, Olga! This is the kind of thing that happens to people like us. I don't know you yet, but I know that whether you're military or pro-tsar or pro-German or just wealthy, you're a target. If you and your mother won't come with me, at least let me try and save your sister from this carnage." He stares intently at what must've been a shocked but still dubious expression on my face. Yet I know he is right.

"She will go with you," I promise.

But it is all happening too fast.

Upstairs I find Larissa crying on her bed, nearly en-folded by layers of silk and lace I've barely noticed she has been transforming for months into a wedding gown. "Will you take care of the dress until I can send for it?" she pleads.

"Of course, Lara. I'll take care of everything," I assure her, without betraying a hint of doubt. We hug for several minutes, exchanging kisses on both cheeks.

Suddenly I do not want her to go, especially with no idea whether I might ever see her again.

Even if I remain stuck in the past, it occurs to me not for the first time that Grandma Olga never once mentioned having a sister. Either they had a falling out, or something so terrible must've happened that she could or would not speak of it.

We pack a few dresses and underclothes in string bags and other non-conspicuous containers, and before I realize it, she has gone. Out into a dangerous, unpredicta-ble world. Out of my life, perhaps. Out, hopefully, toward a happy and safe life.

 exoecs

On *Pascha* morning, my mother greets me with "Christ is Risen!"

"He is risen, indeed," I respond dutifully.

We triple kiss one another on each cheek, and then Mother retreats to her room to pray and read from the Bible and books about the apostles' lives.

After the two of us shred cabbage with pickles and boiled potatoes, I set the lunch aside. With the rest of the vegetables, I plan to make a surprise for Easter dinner: mushroom soup.

In the parlor, I haul out drawing paper and pastels, arranging everything where the tea service once sat. Even though recipes can be located in the bookcase, I can almost recall the ingredients for the things we most likely would've been preparing all week if we had them. Best of all, Lara has spent most of the past several weeks endlessly dreaming aloud of each item: butter, eggs, cream cheese, sour cream, toasted almonds, raisins, currants, multiple spices! My mouth waters at the thought of what we are missing, but I have a task.

Carefully I make a drawing of each item in the recipe, then carefully slice around them as if cutting out paper dolls. As much as I hate to waste flour, I've used a little to concoct a paste that I use to attach each cutout to another large piece of paper.

Then it is time to trace the egg custard itself, which

resembles a pyramid with its top cut off to represent Jesus's tomb. Forced at last to consult one of the now precious cookbooks, I trace and cut out the paper candles separately, as well as the decorations: flowers, a cross, traditional Cyrillic symbols, and tiny letters that form the initials for "Christ is Risen" in Old Church Slavonic.

The "real" vanilla and candied fruits Lara saved I will use in the sweet *kulich* bread—shaped like a church rotunda—that I am going to bake later when I make the soup.

Through the windows, opened on the first day of April to air out the house in spite of the chill, drift the distant sounds of a band playing the French military anthem, "The Marseillaise." To drown it out, I sing aloud to myself—hymns that I somehow seemed born knowing.

Finished at last, I return to the kitchen to locate the one egg we've been hoarding all week. It takes a bit longer to hunt down the red onion and beet peelings Larissa had saved even longer. Dropping everything into the pan, I dismiss my guilt at lighting the gas stove for such a small meal. The stove's six burners and multiple ovens have been almost unused over the past weeks, and there is only enough gas left for another meal or two.

I wait the prerequisite amount of time for the peelings and egg to boil before removing the egg in its bright red new finery.

Much later, I carefully place the posters of the frosted white *pashka*, the bread, the egg, and the cabbage meal into a large wicker "Easter basket" retrieved from Larissa's closet. Especially proud of my festive-looking paper *pashka*, I move slowly toward my mother's drawing room.

There is no priest to bless us or the "food" or the breaking of our fast, but I feel at peace nonetheless. And when Mother sees it, I hope she does, as well.

Chapter 9

Our peace lasts several weeks, with each of us taking turns dressing in servants' clothes and going out into the streets to forage for food and wood.

Fortunately, the weather has warmed considerably, and something resembling normalcy has returned to Petrograd, although it is still a dangerous city for people of our class. Yet it is a relief to get out into the streets once again, even to shop for turnips, in spite of the risks.

Lacking servants, we spend our days cleaning, mending, preparing meager meals, and finally—after all my formerly futile urgings—packing. Packing for what and where we do not know, but we do know that we will not leave until we hear something from or about my father.

Mother wants to go to the British Embassy to ask if they can assist us in getting out of Russia, but we have heard there is a temporary moratorium on that—except for the vast network of members of the Romanov family.

I find I actually miss the tea ladies, as our cleaning and packing breaks are spent putting together puzzles and taking turns letting each other win at dominoes. With our fur muffs and what little yarn and wool we have left, we fashion ourselves scarves, stockings, and hats until the tiny fire sputters out and the lights run out of fuel. Electricity comes and goes. Suddenly the house seems enormous for two people, and we close up several more rooms to conserve heat and light.

Phone lines have long since stopped working, and rarely does anyone show up. When we do hear a knock, we vacillate between hope that it will be my father and fear of what harm might await us from the other side of the door.

Other than going out for supplies, we seldom leave the house, although twice we attend church. Since the Our Lady of Kazan is close by, we go there to pray and seek news. Most churches remain open, which I suspect they will not for much longer. Inside, although the mood is somber, the crowds continue to come—perhaps as much for warmth as worship.

We wear simple cotton rather than expensive chiffon scarves that keep us from standing out, and my weeks of patrolling streets for supplies have yielded us two red armbands that demonstrate our supposed solidarity with the provisional government.

In spite of our "disguise," a few old friends recognize us, and we stand beside one another at the icons, talking in low whispers that may be mistaken for prayers. In this way, we learn that most of the nobility have either been arrested and sent to Siberia or, in some cases, even to refill the cells of the recently emptied out Peter and Paul Fortress. Others have fled the city or even Russia.

"Go to Finland, and from there to Paris," one of our former tea guests urges us. "That's where many are fleeing. You must, too, before it is too late. They are hunting us like exterminators chasing rats. Russia is no place for the nobility right now."

Things seem little improved under the provisional government, with lines nearly as long as before, although the protests have subsided somewhat. Still, it is clear that, instead of a government or a monarchy, it is bedlam that will reign for some time. I *know* that another revolution is coming, and that Lenin will go from making speeches to seizing control, but I cannot remember if it will happen in October or November. Soon, though, and I am convinced my mother and I have to decide what to do before someone decides for us.

One afternoon, dressed in the redesigned remnants of one of my satin gowns, a pair of father's boots stuffed with cloth to make them fit, and my ubiquitous checked scarf, I pass one of the palaces where we had tea a few times only months ago: Countess Shoblonsky's palace, I recall.

Several obviously poor people hurry in and out, and, on a whim, I decide to go inside. No one stops me, and I try to look around and yet still appear as if I belong here.

As near as I can tell from all the marble, gilding, and parquet floors, it is the place I remember. But it has been converted into what appears to be a labyrinth of sleeping quarters. Tapestries nailed to ceilings divide what used to be a parlor into separate "residences" where people sit or sprawl on planked cots or on the floor.

Following the foot traffic and ignoring the chattering of what seems to be multiple families, I make my way up the winding staircase to where I know there are—or were—the family's private areas and bedrooms. Up here, things are arranged much the same as downstairs. In one area, a man roasts sausages in the marble fireplace. Here in this common area, people talk over glasses of tea, voices overly loud as each appears determined to out talk the other. Most conversations involve squabbles over space or bathroom rights, but many are debating politics and the merits of one party or another of the multiple factions that have emerged.

As I wander the circle that leads from room to room upstairs, I again discover areas sectioned off with blankets, pieces of furniture, or monogrammed sheets. No one pays me any attention, and I take a seat near one of the fireplace rooms that seems to be the most popular gathering place. A woman puts a glass of tea in my hand, and I smile gratefully. I still haven't gotten accustomed to the Russian way of drinking tea from a glass rather than the fancy English teacups my mother and the other noble ladies favor.

"I don't care, I'm not going back to work," another woman complains to the room in general. "Who's in a hurry to go back to spending fifteen hours a day, six days a week, at a loom?"

"You'd be lucky *if* they reopen to have a job." Another woman laughs harshly. "The great Kerensky doesn't know his…" and she utters some words I do not completely understand, but do know are expletives.

"Excuse me," I interject casually when a lull falls in the conversation. "Do you happen to know where the woman who originally lived in this palace is? I don't know her name, of course, but she was—"

"She was a damned aristocrat, you mean?" a man interrupts.

"Yes. *Bourgeoisie*," I manage to make the word referring to the wealthy owners of the nation's resources sound as if I have spat it out.

"Who knows?" A few shrugs come at the same time.

"And who cares?" a woman asks. "I get to use her damn fancy pillowcases to warm my feet is all I know." She lifts her foot to reveal a slipper carelessly sewn from linen.

"Best she's in the fortress locked up with the rest of

the enemies of the people," the woman who served me the tea adds.

"Speaking of being locked up, did you hear that damn baby crying all night down the hall? I'd like to lock up its mother for not keeping it quiet!" a man mutters, and the conversation smoothly moves to a litany of complaints about fellow inhabitants—or tenants—of the palace.

At an opportune time, I mutter thanks for the watered down tea, which gets a shrug, and I manage to slip away and back downstairs.

I can hardly wait to get home and tell my mother what I have seen, although each time I come around the corner, I fear what I will see outside—or inside—our house. Both of us now use the servants' entrance, and keep the drapes always drawn and the doors and windows locked. I have one door key, which I use to slip inside after checking the canal-front to ensure no one is watching.

Thankfully, mother is sitting in her boudoir re-hemming another gown she has torn up and refashioned into a modest dress for one of us.

"Don't you see?" I ask after I've told her what I've discovered at her old friend's palace. "We could do the same thing, but plan it. Do it on our own terms. Even invite the people to live here that we choose. It's the only way we can avoid having to leave or having a crowd break in here and trash the place."

She doesn't ask what I mean by "trash the place," even though I am speaking English. Sometimes it is difficult to keep my speech free of modern phrases and allusions.

"But it's my—our—house!"

"It's not, Mother. Not anymore. It belongs to the government, or the people anyway, and if we don't try to do something ourselves—or flee now—who knows what could happen to us! This way we'll be good Soviets or Bolsheviks or Comrades or whatever we're supposed to be now."

My mother trembles, and tears fall to the yellow silk she's working on. I sit beside her on the chaise and put my arm around her. "I know it's hard, Mother, but it's the new reality. Things will never be the way they were before. There will never be a tsar again. This will be a democracy, like France and America."

When she finally stops sobbing and dries her eyes on the silk—her failure to worry about the delicacy of the fabric a sign I take that she may be starting to understand—she gives me a look so sad and so bewildered that I want to start crying, too.

"How, daughter, do you know so many things about the future? You seem so sure of yourself and your ideas, and I'm tempted to dismiss them because I think of you as my little Olga. But you're not. Not little, and sometimes—I'm not sure you're my Olga anymore." She almost whispers the last sentence.

"I've grown up a lot, Mother," I say simply and then try to change the subject by getting her involved in my new plan. "Let's start today by moving all the things we think we cannot live without into one area—the area we choose to keep as our part of the residence. After all—" I force a laugh. "—we should get first pick of living quarters."

Chapter 10

Over the next several days, we work so hard we're too exhausted to look for food. My bedroom, the adjoining bathroom, and my closet get chosen for our living area, primarily due to the fireplace, view of the canal, and quieter location than some of the rooms near entrances and the kitchen. Those I presume will end up as communal areas. That, in fact, is what I have in mind—a commune, of sorts, consisting of miniature apartments occupying each room on each floor. I shudder at the vision of people nailing sheets into the walls, and decide rather than give them a choice of how to arrange their living space, we'll section off the house ourselves. Like an apartment landlord would do. Maybe that makes us true *bourgeoisie*, but I cannot bear to see a repeat of the arrangements of the palace I visited.

We store boxes of our favorite possessions, photographs, and icons in my closet, now nearly empty of wide formal gowns, jewelry armoires, and hat boxes. A pile of items for the use of our new "tenants" or fellow residents we keep boxed up in the main living room, which we have decided should serve as a common area. These include blankets, pillows, clothing, dishware, candles, lamps, etc. The luxuries we don't need, like paintings, small sculptures, vases, and costume jewelry, we box up elsewhere in the hope we can sell things if no one steals them first.

Sadly, many of our books have already been used for firewood, but some of our favorites I decide to keep downstairs in case anyone wants to read them. Whether this "library" idea will work—or matter, since it seems that a good percentage of the population is illiterate—I don't know, but do hope that these books, too, don't end up as kindling.

One morning well over a month after Larissa and Pavel fled to the countryside, the door pounding intensifies. I open it hesitantly to greet a small group of people brandishing brooms, pieces of cobblestone, and planks of wood. Instinctively, I know why they are here and what they intend to do with their make-shift weapons.

As scared as I am, I have rehearsed this moment for days, and I speak before they get too many words out.

"Comrades, welcome. Are you here for the living areas? They have room for several more families, but I'm sure you've heard or you wouldn't be here. I expect the house will be filled by the weekend." I intentionally soften my accent, which I know marks me as an aristocrat, and keep my demeanor gruff but polite. I am dressed down as much as possible, and holding a twig broom in my hand, as if I have been cleaning and might be a former servant. "It's very comfortable, and I'm sure you'll like it. No families with more than three children, though," I add.

"What living areas?" a woman pipes up from the back.

"The ones that belong to the people now, of course. But not all the people in Petrograd can live in the exact same house." I force a laugh. "This one's quite nice and less crowded than some I've seen."

"You live here?" a young man in a frayed coat demands.

"I do *now*," I reply. Before anyone can directly ask me who I am, I hurry on: "Well, do you need a space to live in, or are you just taking up my time? I've got cleaning to do to prepare for the new tenants, and I don't have all day to stand in some former rich family's doorway talking. We can't build a new country just standing around."

I must have successfully dumbfounded my audience, since the woman from the back comes forward to stand beside me. "I would like to find a space for me and my two daughters. Can I see what you have?"

The man who spoke up, one of only two in a group of females, nods. "Why not?"

Two other women line up behind him, and the rest move off down the street to continue their looting or whatever mischief they had in mind.

Inside, I point out the empty rooms that have been, as much as possible, filled with a couple pieces of furniture apiece. "The upstairs is full right now," I lie. "Although I hear there might be an opening soon."

"We can *live* here?" the first woman asks breathlessly.

"This is the people's house now, so they tell us, and you're the people, right? This room's right next to the kitchen and two doors from the bathroom. Yours if you want it."

The woman walks into what used to be my father's study and sits on the floor, as if literally squatting. "It's mine. Mine and my daughters', then," she announces firmly.

"Fine. Anyone else interested in one of the rooms they have left?"

The young man decides he'd like to settle in what used to be the recital room, and I apologize to him for the piano. "We can get it moved out if you don't play, but everyone's hoping someone does play it and won't use it for firewood," I tell him.

"I play," he murmurs and stares at me so long I get

nervous and start pushing my twig broom into the corners. He's incredibly handsome, with dark brown hair, eyes black and shiny as obsidian, and a well-groomed mustache. Only his tattered clothing, worker's hat, and scuffed boots with worn heels mark him as a worker or peasant.

"Fine. I'll see if anyone has sheets for this couch. I'm afraid that's all we have for a bed."

"Fine," he fires back, as if mocking me, but this time he smiles.

In spite of my nervousness, I cannot help smiling back.

I hurry back then to discover that the other women have staked out rooms for themselves and presumably their families. "No more than five to a room, they say," I tell them, and they nod agreeably. I keep using the anonymous "they" when I have any rules to report, as if relaying them from some invisible leader.

"Are you sure the upstairs is full?" the last lady asks. "All my life I've dreamed of looking down on the city. It's just me and my husband. We don't need much space."

As if on cue, my mother descends the staircase in her "new look," moving determinedly toward the front door as if she lives upstairs and is going out for the day.

"Anna," I stop her. "Before you go to work, do you know if those people who were here yesterday are taking that other room overlooking the canal?"

Mother plays her part beautifully. "Don't know, but if they aren't back by this time, I'd say it belongs to the people who take it first."

The woman—who is really not much older than myself—follows me upstairs and I lead her to the room next to ours. My mother and I have already agreed to be careful about who will live in that room—Larissa's old bedroom—as we don't want it to be someone too noisy or too nosy. I have no idea whether I've chosen well, but I want that room occupied soon—and two people, provided they don't argue or drink heavily—would be preferable to a family with kids. I've kept all the empty rooms' doors shut to lend credence to my lies about the upstairs' availability.

"I'm Katya," she says, introducing herself, and instinctively gives me a hug. "Tell whoever's in charge thank you, too." Then, appearing worried, she asks if she should stay here overnight in case that other family shows up for the place. I assure her it's not necessary and that while she goes to find her husband, I'll guard the room for her. I refer to it as an "apartment," although I'm not sure which terminology I should use.

Over the next few days, the mansion looks like I imagine a college dormitory looks on move-in day. People come and go, toting rugs, cots, wooden crates filled with clothes, string bags with meager food supplies, and a few children. Two families show up with cats, and I gently try to talk them out of their pets, although I know it's futile.

And, judging from the amount of "junk" moving in with the new tenants, it might not be a bad idea to have our own resident mouse-chasers.

Thankfully, no one asks about paying rent, since I have no idea how the system is supposed to operate. Will the government just "give" them the spaces, or are they supposed to pay the government something? And if so, to which government do they pay? I shrug, assuming someone will eventually show up and take control away from us. But by then, we will at least have arranged things so that we can manage to live somewhat comfortably and fairly.

Dmitri, our first male "roommate," makes himself incredibly useful, helping to distribute materials and move furniture room to room as needed. Many of the china cabinets make excellent cupboards, as well as provide extra noise barriers. He also saws up some planks acquired from who knows where to make additional cots.

The place hums with activity, and surprisingly, no squabbles—thanks in no small part to the kitchen privileges system that one woman, Marina Ivanovna, establishes within a day of her arrival.

Within three days, two more contingents of would-be looters show up, but a third group has actually arrived because they heard we had living space available. The former servants' quarters in the back fill last, and within four days, we are a full house.

Mother, too, seems to be adapting, finding a fellow

domino player and some ladies who like to sew to chat with in the common room downstairs. Occasionally, however, when I awaken to hear a baby cry or a door shut, I hear her crying softly from her bed next to me.

Chapter II

Every time I see him, he smiles. Dmitri. I love the name. I love the smile. I find myself anticipating the next time I will see him come home or leave. The next time I will pass him anywhere in the house. The next time I will happen to be in the kitchen when he is and we exchange a few pleasantries.

Perhaps I have been too obvious in my return smiles, since after supper one summer evening, he invites me to take a walk. I don't ask mother for permission, which maybe I am supposed to do. Or at least *was* supposed to before our society and all its rules were turned upside down a few months ago.

We stroll to the park beside the nearby Admiralty, then past it and the giant sphinxes that guard the Neva, and on to a bench near the red granite rostral columns dedicated to Russia's four greatest rivers.

I put aside all thoughts of possible danger from the Germans, who so far have not penetrated this far north. Being with Dmitri feels somehow safe.

At first, we chat casually about the city and the other tenants of the house, and I am totally relaxed when he suddenly turns to face me on the bench. "I know who you are," he stares at me as if trying to pierce a light from his eyes into mine.

I swallow hard, unsure if he means what I think he does. "I know who I am, too." I force myself to laugh lightly.

"No, Olga—" He reaches out and puts one hand over mine. "I mean I know that you once lived in the house where we all now live."

Fear? Terror? Is that what I'm supposed to feel? But surprisingly I feel almost relief. "What makes you say that?"

"I think I knew it the first time I saw you wielding that ridiculous broom on the steps." He smiles, the area around his eyes crinkling into the beginnings of a delightful small accordion of creases. "It's fine, Olga. Really it is. I have no plans to tell anyone because—"

"And how do I know that, exactly?" Now my hands do start to tremble, but I'm not sure if it's from fear or something else—like the fact that Dmitri has one of his own hands resting so close to mine.

"Because, for one thing, I'm not who I said I was, either."

"You're not a former soldier?"

"Well, that part is definitely true, unfortunately. I spent a good deal of time in a hospital near the front recovering from a stomach wound. I mean the rest."

"I don't understand. Then who are you?"

"I guess I can tell you part of it."

I draw myself up straighter on the bench. "I should think so, if you're going to sit here and threaten to reveal my identify and maybe get me—and my mother—shot."

"My God, no! That's the last thing I'd ever do." Now he earnestly takes one of my hands in his and gently turns me toward him. "Listen to me. I'll tell you what I haven't told a soul, if you can promise to keep my secret, too."

I swallow again, staring back at the glittering needle-like spire of the Admiralty. "I promise. Of course."

He starts to talk then, at first quickly, but then more slowly, looking me straight in the eyes so that I fear I may melt in them before he finishes. But I do listen, with increasing horror, as he tells of his struggle to get back to his home in Moscow on foot, and eventually of the murders—by both sides—of soldiers and civilians he witnessed.

"And then I found our palace—or what used to be our palace."

This part brings me back to my senses. For a few minutes, I had felt like a love-struck teenager, which seems to be exactly how I'm acting. "Your *palace*? You're an aristocrat?"

"Guilty as charged. A 'minor' one, as they say, but my family has—had—plenty of money and privileges in Moscow society. That was the problem, you see. They did to our home what you apparently tried to prevent from happening to yours. They gutted the interior, and chased my family out. At the time, I had no idea where they had gone, but I started trying to find out from anyone who would talk to me without trying to have me arrested."

Thinking his parents and sister might have gone to their country home well outside of the turmoil in the city, he started walking. "It took me days, but as I worked my way through the forests and got closer, I kept hoping that they were there." His face twists with something like pain. "Be careful what you hope for."

I sit silently, afraid to ask, just waiting as he sucks in deep breaths and then at last continues. "They were there. Or at least their bodies were. The dacha was burned to the ground, but they took the time to drag my parents and sister outside and bludgeon them to death."

He cannot go on, and I sense that he has not previously allowed himself to deal with the horror of that day and what happened.

"They dumped all three of them in my mother's garden." His hands tighten on mine so that I dare not move, and I cry quietly, facing him. At last, I loosen my hand

and offer him the edge of my shawl to wipe his own tears.

"I'm so sorry. I never meant to break down like that in front of you—in front of anyone. I buried them in that damn garden, but now I'm sorry I did. I should have moved their bodies to someplace beneath a large tree."

"You're afraid that someone might—do something to the garden?" I ask hesitantly, unable to comprehend the mental strength it must have taken to dig holes to bury your entire family.

"No! It's just that once I left, once I started heading all the way to Petrograd on foot, I had a lot of time to think about things. Before I got that far, I met a former neighbor who told me it was the servants—*our* servants—who burned the house down and killed my family. It makes sense to me now—the garden, I mean. My mother loved that garden, and she and my sister Tonya used to sit on the bench in the sun and watch the servants plant and hoe and weed. They never thought about helping. None of us ever did. Can you imagine? We just took it for granted that some people worked, and the rest had people work for them. That, at least, is one of the many things I've learned in the past couple of months."

"You're right about the workers, Dmitri, but that didn't give anyone the right—doesn't give anyone the right—to massacre the people who—"

"Enslaved them? Because, basically, that's what we did to the serfs and then the commoners. No, I'll never forgive them, but this country is so confused and angry, and we did a lot to help make it that way. That much I do know. I've seen too many of the tsar's troops massacring innocent, starving protesters on his imperial orders. It's just that I think they threw my family's bodies there intentionally as a message, some sort of symbolic revenge."

I shudder again, thinking about how people Dmitri's family trusted had hated them so much they would toss their bodies into their own garden.

"Enough, my dear young lady. I don't want to *think* anymore. I've had plenty of time to do that, but apparently not quite enough to dull the pain. I'm sorry to unburden myself on you."

"It is not a problem, Dmitri. It helps me to understand things, too. But my sister—"

"You have a sister?"

"Yes. Her name is Lara. She's fled to her fiancé's country home outside Tsarskoye Selo. I thought maybe they would be safe there—and please God—let them be. But now I wonder."

He replaces his hands on both of mine. "I'm sorry. I didn't know, and if I did perhaps I wouldn't have told you my story. Yet I cannot imagine the same thing has happened at every country estate."

As I try to pull my hands away to cover my face, he stops me. "In fact," he says urgently, "I know it didn't. Remember that I walked all the way from Moscow to Petrograd. I saw all sorts of houses and palaces standing, as well as all kinds of people walking and wandering. We're a lost country right now, Olga. Everyone has to find a new direction, and discovering which way to go is as hard for each individual as it is for the government."

"I guess I'm one of the lost, too."

"I don't know. You seem to have a strength in you that's rare."

"For someone my age, you mean?" I know he must be several years older than I, but I don't want him to see me as a girl. Yet I do realize that I feel much older than a teenager these days.

"For someone any age. I've seen a lot of country homes with their original inhabitants and all their servants still working at them, but I've seen a lot of burned-out houses and gutted homes with squatters. Look around us." His arm sweeps back toward the Admiralty Garden we passed earlier, and I turn to look again, at what I've tried to avoid seeing: the homeless people only several hundred yards away. Many huddle under looted mattresses or blankets, but others live beneath feed sacks or pieces of canvas propped up by tree branches.

"Do you know for sure that some of those people aren't from the nobility? Some of them hide—like me—and have nothing left and no place to go."

"I guess I'd assumed they were mostly peasants," I stammer.

"Nothing is what is appears to be anymore," Dmitri says wearily. "That's what I mean by how much I admire the way you took your destiny in your own hands." I turn back to face him as he adds, "I'm glad I know who you are. That you know who I am. It's more than nice to have someone to connect with. To share a common past, even if it's a secret one."

"I feel the same," I attempt a half smile to return his grin.

After all, he doesn't really know *me*. I'm like one of our nested *matryoshka* dolls, layers of identity hidden one inside the other. And the tiniest doll inside—the one that's the most important—is the one I can never share with anyone. *I'm Julie Myers from Euless, Texas, and I'm a high school student from the future—almost the twenty-first century.* That's what I'd like to confess, but instead I wrap my shawl tighter around me and suggest we stroll past the Winter Palace.

Dmitri concurs, since we know mainly government officials use the palace now, and it's heavily patrolled—although mainly by young boys and a battalion of wom-en—and fairly safe. Along the Neva River embankment, I can see it all in one glorious panoramic view: a vast building with white columns, its elaborate facade and balconies rimmed in gold and crowned the entire way by gilded figures from mythology. It seems to stretch for several acres. Across the river, the Peter and Paul For-tress and its cathedral glitter with more golden spires, turning almost blindingly bright as the sun beams down and casts their reflection into the river. We're in the midst of the White Nights season now, so I know it is much later than I would ever be out, but it will stay this light until the wee hours of the morning.

"Have you been across to the island?" I ask, and Dmitri shakes his head.

"I wanted to go. To see the church where the tsars are buried. But I have no desire to get that close to a prison of my own volition."

"Sorry. I hadn't thought of that."

"You must have been there a lot of times over the years, though," he says.

I hesitate. Here comes another nested doll layer: "Not really. We lived outside the city for a long time before we moved to Petersburg—Petrograd, I mean."

"The only place I've been that I really wanted to see again was the Mariinsky Theatre, so I did."

"Really? They let you in like, well, dressed like that?"

He laughs. "Believe it or not, yes. It was when I first arrived in Petrograd, but not that long after the revolution. People were just walking inside, so I followed. There was no charge, and there were actually merchants or workers sitting in the tsar's box."

"What did you see? My mother kept talking about bringing my sister and me there when my father gets home, but I guess—"

"It is as splendid as I remember, if you don't count the absence of the royal emblems they stripped off everything. But they opened the performance with the French national anthem, 'La Marseillaise'—'Long Live the Revolution'—which I guess is our anthem now, too. At least. I keep hearing it played on the street."

I should have realized he had a love for music and theater. That he wasn't who he acted like he was. Although he didn't play the piano in his apartment for the first few weeks after he moved in, lately he has been doing so frequently. He plays mostly folk songs that the rest of the occupants like to sing along to, but a few days ago I thought I'd heard some strains of Chopin or another classical composer. For someone of the working class to play the piano should have struck me—or someone—as odd. I tell him so, out of concern.

"Don't think I haven't thought about it," he admits as we sit together on the embankment. "But music has always been such a big part of my life. I couldn't *not* play after weeks of staring at that piano. You must play, too." He puts it as a statement of fact, assuming that I, like most young women of my class, have been trained in all the fine arts.

"Unfortunately, I never did it well. My parents— well, I remember me torturing them to let me stop taking my lessons when I was a little girl. Perhaps my horrible playing tortured them even more, since they agreed."

I startle myself with this "memory," but try to make it sound off-hand. "We should be getting back."

"You're right. I'm sorry to keep you out—and unescorted—so late."

I think—but I'm not sure—that I blush. Girls don't blush much in my own time, and I doubt that I have before. "I suppose the usual rules of decorum and etiquette no longer apply. It seems as if all women are free to go out on their own these days—which is nice, actually."

He laughs and, once again, my heart does a flip at that smile. We walk slowly back home, although I am reluctant to leave the river. I cannot get enough of watching these extraordinarily long nights, when a rose quartz sunset dissolves briefly into a pearl haze, and then reappears as a ruby sunrise without it ever actually getting dark.

After months of waiting for the river's ice to melt and after all the difficulties we've all faced this winter, I feel as if the sight fills a hunger inside. For the first time it also registers just how many hundreds of couples stroll the embankment as if they, too, cannot tear their eyes away from the bejeweled yet surreal scene. There is still a curfew, but, fortunately, no one comes to round us up.

Perhaps I can blame the White Nights for these feelings I'm developing for Dmitri. At least I hope so, because a romance with someone who is actually more than eighty years older than me makes absolutely no sense.

Chapter 12

Sometimes I marvel at the differences between my "old" future life and this one in the past. Although we are luckier than most here, since we have sporadic electricity and running water—both still novelties for some of the new inhabitants—occasionally I find myself missing things like coffee makers, microwaves, and computers. I'd almost kill for a hamburger right now, as well as the freedom to drive Cheryl's car to the mall. But all in all, besides feeling a sense of always needing a shower and never being full from a large meal, I think I've adapted quite well.

In fact, my old life seems rather shallow when I remember how I used to spend my days, and I know I've never before paid much attention to politics or other people's needs. Now we constantly trade not only political and war news, but items we've secured. Inflation continues to soar so much that a small bag of flour can be exchanged for a piece of furniture. Some of the tenants have done just that, selling chairs, footstools, and other small pieces of furniture from their "apartments" to buy food.

One morning, I spend more than I know a factory worker makes in a day to buy two short candles, and from then on, I find myself coolly evaluating everything with an eye for its value on the unofficial or black market.

A few pawn shops remain open, and I have managed to get rubles for some of my jewelry, although the pawnbroker told me when I questioned the small amount I received: "You can't eat the stuff, so that's all it's worth."

As for my mother, she has actually found a job! Although her piano and language skills are considered worthless in the current job market, she managed last week to convince a meat pie maker to hire her. She comes home exhausted and smelling like a grease pit, but somehow she seems proud to be a worker. I never expected that, since the "old" Anna Petrovna has spent her entire life being served.

The truth is, though, that we need money. Badly. Everything costs so much and inflation soars month after month. We have exhausted all our attempts to withdraw money from Father's bank. It's become too dangerous to go back there and try again, so we gave that up when we opened up the house to tenants. I feel as if I should be the one working rather than my mother, but so far my job-hunting attempts have proved futile.

"We have potatoes," Marina announces proudly one afternoon, and within a few hours, someone else has shown up with two onions. Produce has become a bit easier to obtain in the summer than it was, but still these are prizes for our self-proclaimed kitchen supervisor. She keeps a pot of soup simmering on the stove at all times, and just keeps adding to it as people bring things.

In exchange, Marina permits each of us one heaping bowl of soup a day, although it doesn't matter at what time of day or night we eat it. This way workers on all shifts not only contribute everything from beets to a rare sausage, but they can have a healthy meal based on their schedules. Sometimes I wonder when Marina sleeps, since she is always stirring pots or rolling out cheese- or egg-stuffed pies, although she pretends to grumble all the time.

Only my mother, who sometimes steals a bite at work of the little meat pies—*piroshkies*—claims the smells overwhelm her when she comes home.

You would think it would be hot inside the house with all the doors shut in mid-summer, but to my surprise, most tenants keep their doors open all day. When I try to figure this out and explain to mother how grateful I am that we keep ours shut, I discover that, as Grandma Olga once told me, I cannot come up with a Russian equivalent for the word "privacy." It works well in English, but we try to speak Russian all the time now. Only members of the upper class would be fluent not only in English, but in French, the language of court—not to mention German, which the shopkeepers still speak but which remains understandably unpopular.

In late July, Dmitri announces that he, too, has found work. "I'll be helping set type," he explains. "Once the editors found out I could read and spell, they asked no questions. But after all, some of the leaders from all the competing parties are very literate." He names one of the Socialist Democrat papers that prints erratically, and then asks if I'd like to take a walk with him.

Since I practically live to see his dazzling smile these days, I hide my eagerness when accepting. But first, I go to my room and pull on under my dress the special slip I made for going out. It is half brocade—heavy and hot but sturdy—and half taffeta. Should someone remove my dress in the event I am arrested—or worse—the only thing visible would be a somewhat fancy undergarment with a thick hem. Inside the hem, I have sewn the amber beads, as well as a few of our most valuable jewels. Sadly, I got the idea from recalling what will be the eventual fate of the tsaritsa and her daughters, whose jewel-stuffed undergarments temporarily deflected—or will deflect—their assassins' bullets.

Outside, Dmitri is waiting. As if in mutual agreement, we turn up Nevsky Prospekt and follow it silently until we reach the Anitchkov Bridge, with its four giant statues of stallions pawing the air at each corner. Months ago, hundreds of people died on this very spot when the tsar asserted a last whimper of control and ordered the protestors killed if necessary. Red-coated Cossack guards ran them through with bayonets or sliced them with blades. A more recent protest nearby also failed, the leaders of that rebelling party—including Vladimir Ilych Lenin—have now fled the country, according to the various newspapers that now double as toilet paper.

"Imagine. We are fighting wars abroad and one amongst ourselves at home," Dmitri observes as he takes my elbow to steady me. The streets, now mercifully free of snow, are instead muddy and uneven. Most of the cobblestones and wooden planks have disappeared to be transformed into weapons, building materials, or firewood. Thankfully, the garbage piles have disappeared, although I suspect that this is as much due to people rummaging through them for food and discarded materials than due to an increase in official attempts to dispose of them.

"Except that hardly anyone is fighting the Germans anymore," I note, recalling last month's major losses on the southwestern front. We have heard that initially our soldiers won, but that a major offensive fell apart when entire Russian units refused to fight. We have also heard that so far, 1.5 million of our soldiers have been killed in the war, with another four million wounded and two million prisoners of war.

"All they have left to fight are children. Really, Olga, that's what they are. Poor boys from rural areas who've been handed a rifle but no bullets, or boots, or sometimes boots and bullets, but no rifle. They don't even have gas masks half the time. It's like sending them to the slaughterhouse," he observes sadly. "The boys have to wait for one of their comrades to get killed so they can get their own supplies."

"Will you go back to the front eventually?"

"I don't know. I suppose I should, but I am sure I will be recognized. After all, I had command of my own small unit, and if, praise God, some of my men survived, they would probably turn me over to the authorities. There is a commission now—called the Thirteenth Section—that has been investigating everyone connected in any small way to the tsarist regime. I doubt that I would be of interest to them, though my father might've been if he had—if he had lived. On the other hand, perhaps I have an obligation—"

"But you were discharged when you were wounded, right? Surely, you don't need to go back. You have served your country well, and now you're serving it in a different way at the newspaper."

"Perhaps." He looks curiously down at me as we find a seat on the Fontanka embankment. "You're too wise for your age, Olga Sergeievna."

"Perhaps," I say, and we laugh together. It feels good to laugh again, and I realize that I have been too nervous and worried for the past several months to do much of that.

"Perhaps," he switches to French, but quietly so that no one will hear him speaking it, "someday I will entrust you with the rest of my secrets."

"There's more? More than all the awful things that have already happened?"

"Only that my real name is not Dmitri. I will tell you what it really is one day, but for your own safety, it's best that you don't know in case anyone shows up for me."

"Well, I hope it's a nice name—not something that sounds ridiculous," I tease him back. I find I am not surprised—I would have done the same thing in his position.

We change back to Russian then, joking about the merits of various names and patronymics—the middle names that identify the names of our fathers. "Please don't let it be Akaky Akakovich, or I swear I'll never talk to you again." I have been re-reading Gogol's stories, including the one about a hapless clerk of that name who is obsessed by his overcoat. The name hints at a possible double meaning in Russian that basically labels him as "excrement, the son of excrement."

"Rest assured, my dear comrade, that it is not that."

"How do you like your job?"

A look of almost pain crosses his brow. "Not particularly," he says so softly I have to almost lean in to him to hear. "It's not easy to spend all day working with articles that call for so much change—and death."

"They don't suspect?" I almost whisper.

"No, I've become a good revolutionary to all appearances. Don't forget our old proverb, Olga: 'If you live among wolves, you must howl like one.'"

He gives a low howl, and I laugh, feeling like I could howl myself.

We move slowly along the Fontanka and cross at the Panteleymon chain bridge, anchored by lampposts adorned with gilded double eagles. It is a beautiful summer afternoon, and in spite of all the shortages, geraniums and marigolds bloom in window sills and outside buildings.

I haven't had a boyfriend since I broke up with the one I had last year, and I feel like a teenage girl with a major crush who also finds herself in one of the most phenomenal, romantic cities in the world. But Dmitri—or whoever he is—is a man, not a teenage boy, and I also sense that this is something way more serious than anything I've ever felt. Embarrassed that he might read my thoughts, I chatter on about Lenin and the prospects for his Bolshevik Party.

"He will be back," I say confidently, as if I can predict the future. Which, of course, I can. One thing I know for certain is that Lenin will soon gain control of Russia, and will change history. I wish I could share all this with Dmitri—what will happen when this becomes the Union of Soviet Socialist Republics, the assurance that the Allies will win this war but that there will be yet another world war, and the fact that in seventy years there will be a revolution that will overturn the USSR and turn it into a democratic state.

"I don't know. Some of the editors and writers are firmly convinced he is dangerous insect, now rendered harmless by his absence. Others insist he some kind of savior: the answer to all our prayers for Russia. I wish I could be sure that he *won't* be back."

I can say little, of course, although I suppose when the time comes—if it comes for me—I will act as surprised as I must. As millions of people probably will be.

Once again, it as if I am with Dmitri, but not really with him. This is not me, Julie Myers, but Olga Sergeievna Sheretno, who really doesn't know what her future holds. I am just a warp in time---a half person to him, and I hate that I cannot be myself entirely.

That night I toss and turn in the heat. How can I be in love if I don't belong here? And how dare I even think such a thing when I could be whisked back to the present—hopefully—at any moment? And horror of horrors, how dare I interfere with someone's past? Even with history?

This thought continues to frighten me the most. If I am, in fact, living Grandma Olga's life, what have I already done to change it? Perhaps she and her mother fled their home instead of turning it into a rent-free cooperative. Perhaps they left the country or Olga went to Tsarkoye Selo with Larissa and Pavel. How dare I make all these decisions and try to influence my mother's life, too? What if I have altered things so that Olga never meets her husband and that, in turn, means they never had my grandfather, and thus Cheryl and I were never born? How will I get back home if I don't exist *there and then* anymore?

Once more, I stay awake until nearly dawn, but by then am resolved that I will stop trying to interfere or direct my mother's life. And finally, that I will stop seeing so much of Dmitri.

Chapter 13

One morning I stand in front of the full-length mirror I keep hidden in the closet. I'm totally naked, and although the familiarity of my body soothes me, cannot help notice yet again how thin I am now—not quite emaciated, but definitely too skinny. Staring at Julie's body—not some other one that might belong to whomever I've "inhabited"—always reassures me.

Even if I am some kind of a rudderless vessel, lost in a sea of time, I am the same person who once spent days emptying out Olga's house in Michigan.

I run fingers over the tiny mole I've always had on my thigh. There is a new scar on my knee from hauling wood around the house, but that, too, is somewhat encouraging. At least I am not a ghost of some kind. I am in my same old body, thank God.

Standing sideways, I notice my breasts seem shrunken, and blush to myself when I wonder what Dmitri might think of this body.

In spite of all my resolve, I find I have little will power when it comes to avoiding Dmitri. I seem literally to live for a glimpse of him and a chance to talk with him. Even though I often suggest we stay in the common room and have tea, as difficult as it is to obtain now, I feel as if I cannot survive without his presence in my life. If it turns more serious, I promise myself I will tell him that I just want him as a friend.

Although I think I am exerting some self-control and avoiding him more often, my mother comments on how much time we spend together. "He's a nice young man, Olga, but you really do see more of him than is appropriate." She says this gently but firmly, as if she has rehearsed it many times.

"You're probably right, Mother. I'll try not to be around that part of the house when he is not at work." I don't tell her that I know exactly when he leaves and departs, or that any change to his routine I immediately notice.

"I don't know when the war will end, let alone what is going to happen to our wonderful country, but he is not..." I can see her struggle for the right words, and finish her sentence for her quietly.

"Of our class?"

"Well, yes. I know that things are supposed to be more equal," she stumbles over the last word, "but who knows what wrongs will be righted in the future?"

"I agree," I say reluctantly, adding to myself, *yes, many wrongs will be righted in the future. But not until many more wrongs have been committed.*

෬෬෬

Besides Dmitiri, I have become good friends with my "next door" neighbor, Katya, who works at a glass factory, and is married to Sasha, who has special permission not to be in the military because he delivers mail.

"At least he does when there is mail to deliver and when the people it's addressed to still, well, still live where they used to live," Katya explains. "You cannot imagine how difficult it is trying to locate people these days."

Katya and I are playing a dice game and half listening to the sweet notes of a folk song emanating from Dmitri's room. "Just like all of us living here now," I say lightly.

She smiles and nods, and I realize she does not suspect who I am, only perhaps that I am more educated than some of the other tenants. "Exactly. And since no one seems to know who pays for mail service now, he hasn't gotten a salary since, well, since the revolution."

"My God! How awful for you!" I know Katya works ridiculously hard at the factory, even though the work day fortunately at last has been reduced to eight hours, but I had no idea she was struggling to support both of them. I feel guilty, because in a sense my mother is doing the same thing, although Katya has been trying to get me a position at the glass factory.

"It's all right. He gets all over the city, and some-times people are so pleased to get a letter that they invite him in for something to eat or drink—or slip him some money for ensuring that their mail gets where it should. Last week he brought Marina an entire bag of onions, a cabbage, and even some salt."

"Ah, that explains why the soup tasted even better than usual."

Sasha also keeps abreast of what's going on all the time, and Katya in turn keeps me informed whenever I see her. In August, the tsar and his family are taken to Siberia. Another threatened rail strike and talk of a poten-tial major offensive have the entire city in an uproar. Pet-rograd is supposed to mobilize for an attack by the Kai-ser's troops. Lenin alternatively is reported to be here or preparing to leave or on his way back to Petrograd—which, I finally realized, will soon be named Leningrad in his honor.

"Have you seen all the posters reminding us to wear our gas masks?" she asks, and then shakes her head. "As if we can get our hands on any of them."

The war is just one of the things I try not to think about—along with the immediate future, my sister, Dmitri, my mother's long hours, my father's whereabouts, and the far, far future.

പ്രയ

In September, the weather is already cooling, and I shudder to think of how we will all keep warm this winter. Dmitri seems to be working longer hours, and my mother has come down with a cough. Since the threat of typhoid still has all of us afraid, I insist she stay home from work for several days.

In one of the common rooms and the former scene of so many afternoon teas, I keep an eye on two little girls while their parents go in search of food. Besides volunteering at one of the nearby hospitals a few days a week, I have tried to find ways to be useful to others who live here and have somehow become known as someone to come to if there's a problem or someone needs something.

"Just ask Olga" has become a common enough phrase that it is perhaps not surprising that it is to me Sasha comes that afternoon with a problem.

"I have mail for three people I don't know, but it's all addressed to this address," he explains, passing me three envelopes. "Do you have any idea if this is the right building?"

I can barely breathe when I see the name on one of the envelopes: Anna Petrovna Sheretno. My mother. The other two are addressed to people who now live in the former servants' quarters.

My face feels red and flushed as I try to act nonchalantly. "I think I know them. They live in the back of the building. I can pass these on, if you'd like."

"Please. I've delivered them here, and that's my job, right?"

"It is indeed. Do you have time for tea?" I ask, trying to keep my voice and body from shaking.

"Thanks, Olga, but I have more mail to deliver from headquarters. The war is getting too close, and we may have to stop delivery yet again." He sighs. "See you later."

I excuse myself, warn the girls not to move an inch, and dash upstairs.

Although I can hardly wait to find out whether the letter might be from my father or my sister, and have no way to recognize my father's handwriting—and my memory of Larissa's is faint—my mother is asleep. I know she would rather be awakened for a letter, but her breathing is too ragged for me to want to interfere with her sleep.

Instead, I slide the envelope on the nightstand and run back downstairs to deliver the other two.

છ્ગ્ન

That evening I am finally free to return to what I now think of as "our apartment" instead of our room in our mansion. At first, I think my mother is asleep again, although she sprawls face down across her bed. But then I notice her shoulders heaving, and catch a glimpse of paper poking from under the bed where the letter has apparently fallen.

"What's happened?" I race to her side and put both arms on her back. She shakes her head and dissolves into no-longer-silent sobs.

I reach down and extract the letter she received, glancing quickly for a signature, but see only initials. The first sentences tell me what we did not want to know:

Dear Anna Petrovna:

In the sad event that no one has yet notified you of the fate of your husband, Sergei Ivanovich Sheretno, I feel it is my responsibility to inform you of his death and his great sacrifice for his country and his tsar...

Unwilling to read more, I stop and lie down beside my mother. For now, the circumstances of my father's death mean little. He is gone, and all my mother's waiting and worrying have yielded nothing but an intense grief. Although I had little time to get to know him, other than hearing the many stories my mother has told Larissa and me, I know how devastated she must be at the loss of the man she has loved for over twenty years.

It is the middle of the night when I awaken. My mother has finally fallen asleep. Thankfully, I've saved some aspirin and some laudanum—which no one seems to know or care is actually the potent narcotic opium—and sit patiently in our one chair and wait for morning. A few drops in her tea when she awakens will enable her mind and body to cope a bit better.

Lighting the oil lamp, reluctant as I am to waste any, I read the rest of the letter from the anonymous writer.

Your husband led his troops into a particularly dangerous battle, but at the last minute, half of them retreated from him and the front. He and the rest had no chance, and although no one could say for sure if the bullet that killed him came from a German or a Russian gun, he died in the service of his country. No one could wish for a more honorable death. God bless you and your daughters. He spoke of you all often and missed you more than a man should miss his family.

Chapter 19

Days drift by slowly as mother struggles to deal with father's death. It seems to help her if we talk about him, and one day I discover a little of the history of my amber beads.

"Remember," she asks, "the necklace your father bought you? I haven't seen you wear it lately, but it used to make him smile to see it."

"Which necklace, mother?"

"The one made of amber, of course. The one he said would protect you from yourself. He always worried about you, darling. You're so headstrong and so independent that he feared you'd get yourself in some kind of trouble someday. I must admit, though, that you made him proud. The amber *is* potent, and has protected our people for hundreds or perhaps thousands of years. Even though he gave matching earrings to Larissa, we've never worried about her that much—"

She stops talking and misses a stitch in the shawl she is embroidering.

"Until now, I know."

We've heard nothing from Larissa or Pavel, and every day we half hope, half fear any news. Perhaps she packed her amber earrings, since I did not find them when we emptied her room.

Somehow, I can almost remember my father handing me the beads, telling me that they've been in my family for generations. Almost I have this memory that is Olga's.

For me, the amber *must* work. I am safe. My mother is safe. My sister might even be safe. Every day I find myself sliding the beads out of my petticoat hem and fingering them lightly, not just in the hope that they will somehow whisk me home, but because I am amazed at their warmth, softness, and the way the light fires them shades of tawny, lemon, butterscotch, and caramel.

They also seem to reassure me by their presence. Perhaps it is the beads themselves, nearly each one preserving a bit of flora or a tiny insect, which makes me feel an affinity to the amber. If I look too long, I start to imagine myself as one of them: a miniature time capsule entrapped in the wrong era.

Amber is plentiful and inexpensive here, but to me it

is my most cherished piece of jewelry, and I will not wear it and risk anyone stealing it.

☙ ❧

Although for days we've nearly forgotten about the war and the revolution, eventually my mother returns to work only to find that her job has been given to someone else. So I shouldn't be surprised that when Katya drops by our room in my absence to announce that there is one opening at the textile factory next door to her own workplace, my mother takes it without consulting me.

"Mother, how could you? I am younger and stronger. I should be working and taking care of you."

"No! It is I who has lost my husband and possibly my youngest daughter." She grips my hand forcefully. "I need to be busy all the time now, Olga. All the time. You must let me do this. And besides, I've already worked an entire day. You cannot just show up and expect to take my job away from me!"

I almost laugh, admiring the spirit that she has shown, and cannot help comparing her to Cheryl. But that's not fair, I tell myself. Cheryl never lost everything she owned, but she lost her parents at age seven. She had to be a tough little girl—and later a tough woman. I've only seen her frivolous side, and if I've learned anything from living in the past, it's that human nature is resilient enough to overcome the worst of tragedies—and to handle it with strength. I may have seen the worst of people here, but I've also seen the best of them, and the thought is comforting.

How could I have been so critical of Cheryl—and both of us of Olga? No wonder my great grandmother always appeared so strong and resilient. She endured all this: the sudden poverty, the Revolution, the loss of her position in society and way of life, the hidden identity, the death of her father and presumably at some time in the future her mother and sister. And in the end, she even lost her own country and then, after surviving the Great Depression and a second world war, her own son and his wife.

Olga's obsession with privacy also makes perfect sense now, as at last does all her hoarding. I find myself collecting old newspapers, shreds of cloth, unused bits of candle wax, and pieces of leftover thread. Everything I see has a potential use for my mother and me or for trade value. Even if I didn't know that another wave of this revolution is coming and that our situation could worsen, I cannot bear to see anything go to waste.

In fact, I make so many trips to different pawn shops that other tenants often entrust me with their stuff to sell. The broker at my favorite place never looks askance at me or seems to suspect or even care where the "goods" come from.

Slowly my own jewelry boxes, closets, and boxes of gowns also empty, although the pawn broker pays me only a few rubles for each exquisite gown, and little more for the jewels. I cannot imagine why he wants the dresses, but suspect the silks, satins, and brocades will be cut up for other things.

The hardest day is the one when I must part with the amethyst and diamond pendant I wore to the Alexander Palace, which earns me enough to buy some precious flour. The only things my mother insists we preserve, no matter how much we could get for them, are her icons and Larissa's wedding gown. "We owe that to her," she insists. "No matter what hardships she must be enduring right now, she deserves to know that the one thing she entrusted us with is safe."

Occasionally, I return home to find her sitting with the dress in her lap, stroking the satin and lace, a faraway look on her face. I am not sure at those times if she is thinking of her missing daughter or her own wedding day or her lost husband.

"Shouldn't we save Larissa's own icons for her, too?" I ask, envisioning my sister fervently sitting in front of her own painted religious images and the candlelight flickering on them while she prayed.

My mother still does that with hers, but in the closet where there is no danger of someone unexpectedly walking in or searching our apartment.

"You already packed them, didn't you?"

"No, Mother, I didn't. Perhaps she took them with her."

"I have no doubt that she did," Mother says softly. "I haven't seen her icons since she left, and I cannot believe that I didn't notice they were missing. I am not such a good mother, am I?" Tears threaten to overflow her eyes, and I reach out and hug her to me.

"You are a wonderful mother. To both of us." I feel awkward, as if playing a role in a play once again, but I *have* grown to love my new family. For just a moment I feel guilty about the mother I left in the future, but those thoughts come so rarely now. I know I must live the life that fate—the amber necklace—has dealt me.

ᕕᕗᕔ

In spite of all mother's admonishments and my own reservations, I do not entirely avoid Dmitri. Often he brings us pine branches to boil as a substitute tea, assuring me that this will be good for our health. He is extra solicitous of mother in her bereavement, and I selfishly hope his kindness to me is not primarily because he believes I have just lost my beloved father.

Some evenings when he is not needed to set type or proofread, we sit near his piano while he runs fingers up and down the keyboard and tells me about the lives of his favorite musicians and composers. He speculates that some of them may leave Russia—or may have already went into exile. "Thankfully Stravinsky is stuck in Switzerland. How can anyone live and work here? They would have to compose or perform in trade for flour or eggs."

But it is really the music of *his* voice that gives me the most joy.

Other times I watch him whittle at pieces of wood, or beams, or wainscoting that once adorned various rooms in our mansion. He enjoys carving things that tenants need, from chairs and benches to cradles and tables. The recipients are more than happy to bring him additional pieces of wood—stolen, I suspect, from other mansions or palaces—but he never questions the source.

"I cannot believe I can do this," Dmitri says one evening, sounding awed. "Who would have ever guessed a soldier and a member of the nobility could be turned into a craftsman!"

"Shhh." I glance around what serves as the community parlor nervously. In his enthusiasm, Dmitri sometimes forgets to be cautious. That would surprise me if I weren't the one actually keeping two lives a secret—my real one in the future and my real identity as a member of the nobility—in order to protect my third one as a member of the working class.

I nearly laugh aloud at Dmitri's guilty look, and consider asking him to make me a *matryoshka* doll so I can keep track of all my identities nested inside of identities.

As if reading my thoughts, he asks, "What can I build for you, my sweet Olga?"

"Nothing. You know that I already possess more

than most people." It still pains me to observe all the hat-less, coatless, and shoeless men, women, and children on the streets. If the upcoming winter is as treacherous as last year's, most of them will suffer frostbite or worse.

"So nothing for my beautiful lady," he murmurs without taking his eyes off the wood chisel someone traded him for a chicken that he, in turn, had traded someone else for in place of some purloined ink from the newspaper. I'm grateful he is not looking at me, for once again I feel my cheeks grow warm and probably flushed with color.

Sometimes I wonder what he sees in me—not just in-tellectually or emotionally, but physically. The mirror, which I wish weren't too large to cart away and pawn, does not reveal a "beautiful lady" as much as a haggard-looking stranger with too prominent cheekbones. My dresses hang more loosely every week. Bones seem to strain against the skin over my rib cage, and I feel guilty over all the times Tiffany and I used to make a big pro-duction out of dieting so we'd look great in our bikinis. I remember reading at the library about how fat was once a sign of wealth, and now I understand. All around me people wear an almost skeletal, pained expression. A look of hunger.

Mother, too, gets skinnier by the week. Often some-one has overturned one of the scarlet trams that provide the major method of city transportation, so she has to walk all the way to or from the factory.

"Sometimes they just remove the driver and take his ignition key," she complains. "I'd like to carry around one of my long sewing needles to give someone a good poke! Imagine trying to disrupt the travel of decent, hardworking folks. The revolution is over! This makes no sense."

I almost laughed when she called herself "decent, hardworking folk," recalling all too well the woman who only a few months ago hosted formal teas wearing impeccable afternoon gowns and ordered around a bevy of servants. I have to give her credit: she's grown tough as granite even though she's become thin as a cattail.

In spite of our weight losses, at least neither of us bear scars, the way so many on the street do. Some bear old bayonet wounds or have been hit in the face by flying stones. Sasha has a mark on his face left over, he admitted to me, from this winter's riots when people threw poorly aimed chunks of ice at the police and soldiers.

I do grasp how lucky I've been on my forays around the city. Nothing awful has happened to me. And although I have not yet become immune to the frequent sight of a body curled up alongside a building, I confess to being thankful someone seems to come and pick up the dead each night. The first time it happened—the first body I saw—I tried to help the person, not realizing until I touched the woman on her arm that she was dead, rather than only injured or passed out. It was then that I had my worst day in the past, crying to myself in my longing to be back in the future: back in Great Grandma Olga's house instead of her past life.

Other days race by, and I find myself almost forgetting I do not belong here. I babysit for one of the tenants, try to convince Marina to let me stir a kettle of stew, scrub the tracked-in mud from the common area, help out at the nearest hospital, share dinner with my mother, and spend evenings talking with Dmitri or Katya. Yet although I care about them both, I often long to just be alone, without tenants, without servants—just alone with a cup of tea in the house.

When afternoons surrounded by so many people get me crazy, I take walks. Not even all the sadness, desperation, war, and hunger on the streets can mar Petrograd's beauty. I begin to wonder if I do, indeed, as Great Grandmother Olga once assured me, "have Russia in my soul."

Chapter 18

I am carefully shredding the last of my dresses into hospital bandages one afternoon when Dmitri knocks on our room door. He stands awkwardly in the hallway, wondering if I might like to get some fresh air. Of course, I accept.

Indian summer has arrived, and the effect of scarlet, orange, and yellow leaves against the city's plentiful gold spires and cupolas is breathtaking. For the first time, Dmitri holds my hand while we walk, and I squeeze his back. I feel like shouting with happiness.

That feeling dissolves instantly when Dmitri announces, "I may have to leave soon, *mon cherie*."

"What do you mean? Go back to the front?"

We are sitting on the ground in what used to be the

tsar's Summer Garden, since all the benches that aren't stone have been stolen for firewood. Instead of a park, however, it resembles a combination homeless shelter and training ground now.

"There or to some other city where I can get work."

"But what about the newspaper? You said they love your work."

"They do. Perhaps too much. That's the problem. Even though Lenin has fled the country, he keeps track of everything going on here from Finland. And he has taken a liking to my editing. Both he and some other fiery revolutionary named Trotsky think I am some kind of mental giant because I pretend to agree with them. Earlier this summer, when Lenin had the time to come in and out of the newspaper office, he took an interest in me. He may not know who is writing or editing which pamphlet or article right now, but my sources whisper that he may be back in Petrograd any day. He may be here now in secret, for all I know. But I can't do it, Olga. I cannot betray what I believe in to help him overthrow my country's government yet again."

"No, of course not. But you said you believed in self-government for the people, not in the old system. How is Lenin much different?"

"What he wants is more radical than anything I can imagine for Russia. He wants to exert too much control over the people he claims to want to represent. I've told you that I fear his ideas sometimes, although I also admire some of them. I just do not want to be a part of it. Not of the revolution he wants to start again."

"I understand, I guess." We are still holding hands, and suddenly he bends over and brushes my forehead with his lips, which are surprisingly warm in the coolness of the day.

"Not to mention that I seldom get paid. And there's something else. I don't want to leave you, Olga. That's my problem. Before I worried only about my own survival, but now I worry about yours and your mother's, too."

"We're fine," I say bravely, but inside I am anything but brave. How can I bear to lose him?

"You would be fine if you came with me," he murmurs, reaching out as if to stroke my hair.

"Come with you?"

"Yes, to another city. Perhaps…Well, I must tell you what has been happening since I made up my mind to leave the newspaper. I have a job opportunity, Olga. It is only an apprenticeship, but it is with an associate of one of the most talented furniture making families in Russia. But they are talking about leaving. Some already have, as they once had a lot of imperial commissions. It means I would have to go, too—farther from the front, but safely away from the revolutionary headquarters. Perhaps to the north, close to Lake Ladoga." He stops and stares deeply into my eyes. "Closer to Finland."

When I respond with no more than a startled, "Oh," he continues: "I cannot live like a member of the nobility anymore. There is no room in the new Russia for my kind." He pauses and brushes a hair from my face. "Nor for yours, my darling. I know I am not being a good Party member, but I cannot envision a life in the factory for you or for your mother."

"Dmitri, we will manage. I will find work, and mother will get a better position." But my heart is not in my protests. This is not the Russia we knew, and while I agree that the nation's riches must be shared more equally, I admit to being tired. And my mother is even more weary.

As if to verify my doubts, my stomach rumbles with hunger.

"I heard that!" he says, frowning. "Olga, this job could turn into something permanent if I become associated with the Meltzer family. They are giving me an opportunity to work with my hands. To fashion pieces of furniture more elaborate than the chests I have made for the tenants. And I love it. I truly do."

"The Meltzers? Of course, I've seen their store on Bolshaya Morskaya. Is it still there?"

"Not exactly. But the family is intact, and there will be others—perhaps not in Russia—who have need for their talents. I've shown one of my small chests to their associate, and he thinks I show 'promise.' He is even willing to share some of their tools with me!"

His eyes and entire face glow with more than the cold, and I realize again how happy he seems while fashioning a new chair or bench for someone. He really does adore creating furniture, and the piece of me that is still Julie must admit that, in all actuality, there will be no future for him as a landowner and nobleman, let alone a soldier.

"You should do it then. You have a tremendous amount of skill." I stop and bite my lip because I almost added, "darling."

Now his eyes are all about me, and I can tell he has stopped thinking about making furniture. "Olga, let me take care of you—and Anna. At least let me try."

I am touched that he cares, and infinitely relieved that he doesn't plan to walk out of my life. And beyond that I sense a resurgence of that overwhelming sense of happiness I felt earlier, but now tinged with outright delight. It is the feeling, I realize, of finding out that someone you love feels the same way. Even though he has not yet put it into words, I know that he loves me.

"Olga, I promised one day I would tell you who I am. And I would not expect you to just leave your life here without knowing my true name. It is—"

I put my finger to his lips. "You don't have to. I would go with you anywhere."

We are now oblivious to the world around us. To the half covered statues. To the make-shift homeless shelters. To the boys doing military training exercises. To other couples. To workers hurrying to and from their jobs.

"Are you certain?" he asks earnestly. "This might *not*

work out. They may not think I am good enough or I may not learn all that is expected of me. And we may not have comfortable accommodations. But yet I need you, Olga. I love you! And I don't expect your mother to see me as I am, at least not yet, but I would never dishonor you—or your father's memory. I want you to marry me, Olga. Here, in Petrograd, before we leave."

I am stunned. Both of me—the future and the present me. I am only seventeen, although I realize that now my eighteenth birthday—Julie's birthday—came and went this summer.

"I don't know. I mean, I'm too young for marriage. But perhaps there is still a way we can go with you." I recognize in that instant the headstrong me that my father worried about, the stubborn young lady who would cross the country—and perhaps leave it—to an unknown life with someone she has only known for five months.

"Then it is settled?" His eyes lock mine, and then his lips play with my forehead, my eyes, and my cheeks before he enfolds me in his arms.

I am scared but somehow ecstatic! Stubbornly brushing aside all my doubts about interfering with the future and with Olga's life, I eagerly make plans with Dmitri. We talk for hours. I also go over and over what I will say to my mother, and when—or if—I will tell her that while Dmitri is a member of the working class, he has not always been. Yet somehow, I believe the "new" Anna would approve even if I fell in love with a worker and not a member of the nobility. Class distinctions seem to be fading, even if they may never disappear entirely.

"I am not ready to marry you, Dmitri. But I am not saying I will not. We would find separate apartments at first, of course, and then maybe—" I pause at his crestfallen expression.

"But do you love me?" he persists.

"Yes, darling, I do. But right now I have to think of my mother, and it seems so selfish to worry about our own happiness." At the same time I am saying these words, I cannot believe myself. For months, I have lived to see Dmitri, to talk to him, to stare into those intent black eyes.

What is holding me back? Practicality? No, it's that I don't belong here and that I cannot make choices with someone else's life.

Dmitri sighs, but forces a grin. "For now that is enough. I will wait for you. But I do believe we must get out of the city soon. If not the country. As long as you agree that you and Anna will come with me, I will be content with that."

The sun is setting behind the Admiralty as we head back to our apartments. Just before we go around the corner where our fellow tenants can see us, Dmitri stops and twirls me in the air, lifting me down and at kissing me on both cheeks. I can barely stand to have him move away from me as we walk toward the entrance.

Once at the closed door, he leans over and kisses my

hands, then whispers in my ear. "It's Ivan. Ivan Kuznetsov."

He strides happily away along the canal-front then, leaving me standing at the door, my mind trying to cope with what he just said and my body still tingling.

I run inside, blindly reaching my room and relieved it is empty. Throwing myself on the same bed where my mother has cried so many tears, I let my own pour out. It's not possible. His name. It cannot be. Olga Sergeievna *Kuznetsov.*

I am madly in love with my own great-grandfather!

Now the hand holding and the kisses, innocent as they were, embarrass me. How could I have? How could this have happened? Is it what really happened to Grandma Olga? Is this how she finally met her beloved Ivan? Of course, she loved him. He is phenomenal!

But he is—or will be—hers, not mine. I don't have the right—and suddenly it all seems horribly wrong.

Thank God nothing happened between us, except love. But the word itself makes me wonder if I really did or do love him in a romantic sense. I've turned to him again and again for solace. He is older and wiser than I. Almost since the first day I saw him I have felt a connection between us. Yet was this *that kind* of love, or more of the kind of love I might have felt for an older relative?

Nevertheless, this time the beads have not protected me. I lift them out of my hem and stroke them. I need help at this instant. Need to figure out what to do if I am to stay here knowing what I know. Knowing that Olga is *supposed* to marry Ivan, that she must, or I will never exist.

My tears drip onto the beads, and I recall the story my mother told me last week. It is a legend about a beautiful maiden with long, flowing golden hair and cornflower eyes who loved to stroll the beach. One day, imagining she heard music, she felt an intense power that compelled her to wade into the water. As she began to swim, however, a vicious whirlpool sucked her in and pulled her to the bottom, where the Prince of the Seas captured her. This prince inhabited a magnificent underwater palace of glowing amber; he instantly made the maiden his bride, imprisoning her in his golden home.

Although she lived in a sumptuous home fashioned with pieces of amber that formed everything from the chandeliers to the massive columns and staircases, she could not return the prince's love. When she begged to be released, the prince flew into a rage, lifted her onto his white stallion, and rose with them to the surface amidst a terrible squall. Dressed in a splendid golden gown, she was draped head to foot with amber beads, her lovely blonde hair adorned with an amber crown.

As they emerged from a tumultuous sea, the maiden's parents saw her struggling in vain to free herself. But when the prince and the horse with its two riders sank back into the churning waves, the girl's parents knew they had lost her forever.

In one final, brave gesture, the maiden yanked at her beads and tossed dozens of amber pieces into the sea to demonstrate to her parents how much she loved and missed them.

Now, whenever the Prince of the Sea becomes angry, the sea boils from turbulent storms, but the maiden's amber beads and pieces of her palace float to the shore as a reminder of her loyalty, strength, and love.

It seems odd that Great Grandmother Olga never included this legend in her storytelling repertoire until I realize why she didn't: her own son—my grandparents—drowned. This legend must have resonated too closely.

I finally fall asleep, dreaming of amber princesses and underwater castles that take life away from one unhappy maiden.

Chapter 16

Katya knocks on our door just after sunrise. I glance at my mother's bed, but she has apparently already left for the factory.

"Olga, please!" a desperate cry accompanies the knock.

Instantly awake now, I open the door and pull Katya inside. I realize she has never seen how much better my mother and I live than some of the tenants with smaller quarters, but Katya's tears persuade me none of this matters.

If someone is going to turn us in to the authorities, it is unlikely it would be my new friend. And her distress convinces me it doesn't matter; I have to learn to trust some people.

"Sasha is gone!" she announces, her face wet with tears.

"What do you mean? Isn't he practically always gone?"

"But this is different. It's been many more days than usual, Olga. And usually he gets a message to me one way or another."

"Communication is unreliable and slow now. You, of all people, should know that. Not everyone takes their responsibilities of forwarding mail as seriously as Sasha."

"I know," she says morosely. "You are right, of course. But Olga, I could not live without the man I love!"

Her words bring yesterday's memories pouring back. Dmitri. Ivan. Whoever he is, he is not mine to love. At least not as a husband.

It is then that her words penetrate: "It was difficult enough to lose Papa." She almost starts to relapse into tears, but then looks at me and straightens. "Oh, Olga, I am so, so sorry! How could I complain when grief over your own father is so new?"

My own father? How could I have nearly forgotten so soon? "It is all right, Katya," I assure her. "There are too many things to worry about right now."

"I know, but I have been selfish."

"No, no you have not. I should apologize. I have been too involved with my own troubles to pay attention to those of others."

"*Nyet*, Olga. You are always here for everyone. People notice. They may not always say *spaciba*, but they are thankful!"

Embarrassed, I take her hands in mine. "Katya, tell me about your papa."

"It was many years ago now," she says, waving her hands as if trying to dismiss the past. "But it was another set of strikes. The beginning of what could have been a revolution, so I think about it often these days."

Gradually she does tell me, though. About her father's smile, his dedication to change, his commitment to teaching her how to read in a country that did not value such things, and finally, about his job at a Siberian gold mine. Apparently, there had been a miners' strike back five years ago, and rather than listening to or even disciplining the strikers, the tsar's soldiers had fired on them.

"It was a massacre," she says lowly. "The Lena fields ran with blood instead of gold that day. Over a hundred of my father's co-workers died or were injured with him. My mother's heart failed a few months later, and I know she died of a broken heart, not just a weak one." She stares at the door, which is not thick enough to block the sounds of children dashing around the house trying to trade or sell bits and pieces of string or canvas they have foraged. But she does not really hear them.

When she turns back to me, her beautiful face quivers with fear. "Sasha and I moved here to forget. To find a better life. What will I do now if I have lost him, too?"

I hug Katya tightly, trying not to let her know that I have tears in my eyes not just for her, but for myself.

"Come on," I gently extract her hands from mine. "Let's go to the kitchen and see what Marina is making. Someone brought some more flour and some yeast yesterday, and I heard her chattering about the possibility of making bread again."

Temporarily cheered by this possibility, Katya waits for me to don a plain cotton dress and we hurry downstairs, where the unmistakable, delectable smell of freshly baked bread has the entire building milling about the common area.

Our bellies filled with bread and black currant preserves, Katya and I curl up on the floor and hug one another. At last, we decide to cheer ourselves up and to surprise Marina by walking down Nevsky Prospekt in search of a carrot to contribute to her next stew—or better yet, to drink the carrot tea that has replaced the real thing.

But before we manage to reach the front door, it flies open.

Sasha stumbles in, weary and coated with mud, and Katya leaps the few steps between them. As they wrap themselves around each other, showering one another with kisses, I stand back enviously.

"Where have you been?" Katya finally manages to get out.

"All the way out of the city. Just outside Tsarskoye Selo."

"No wonder you have been away for so long."

Sasha appears shaky and grim. "Now that the Bolsheviks have captured a majority in the Petrograd Soviet, things should get better soon. But the city has had to mobilize once again for the war, and I don't know how we can fight two wars on the same front!"

"Sweetheart," Katya whispers, chewing on her lower lip. "You do not have to save the world. Please do not worry about such things. I have my eight-hour day now. Yes, the coal and bread are still impossible to obtain, but we will survive all this." She sweeps her thin arm toward the windows.

"We *have* to worry about all this, my Katya. Someone must, just like your father did. If the people do not retain control, we will get another blood-sucking, money-grabbing tsar. This cannot happen."

Katya sighs heavily—a sigh I recognize as similar to those of the others living here, including my mother. "You are right, I know this. But who sent you to Tsarskoe Selo?" she asks, attempting to change the subject.

I listen with interest, wondering exactly how soon the provisional government will fall. With rumors of Lenin's return to Petrograd running wild, I fear it will be soon. But soon Sasha nearly sweeps the revolution from my mind.

"First a delivery. And then I had a message from one of the palaces outside the village. They were packing to leave and wanted some things shipped to the city, so I promised to do it for a very large fee. Look!" Out of his pockets, he pulls two jeweled broaches that look oddly familiar.

"But who were these people? Are they nobility?"

"Katya, my darling, it is best if you do not know too much. I probably shouldn't have been there, but right now we need the money—although I don't trust our currency and prefer to take things I can trade for food and warm clothes." He looks down ruefully and our eyes follow his.

"Sasha! Your feet! What happened to your shoes?" Loosely wrapped pieces of cloth have replaced his usually sturdy, though worn, shoes.

"Stolen, my dear. But could we talk about all this later? I really could use a cup—"

"Of tea! Yes, of course, Sashenka." Katya nearly pushes her husband into a chair. I stop her from leaving with one hand and offer to get it for him, although I need to know where he obtained the jewelry that I am almost certain once belonged to our family.

When I return to the common room, they are talking rapidly and quietly, and for some reason wear almost guilty looks as I hand Sasha a glass of tea.

"What is it? Do you need me to get something for your feet, Sasha?" When neither answers, I presume that they want to be alone. Yet I must know about the broaches—and what is happening outside Tsarskoe Selo, the town known as the tsar's city. The city where Lara and Pavel fled. How do I ask?

"I'll just go and see if Marina has some soup," I offer almost reluctantly.

"No, wait," Katya reaches out and touches my arm. She blushes furiously. "There's something we have to ask—or give—you."

"What is it?" I feel my own face flush, as if something awful is about to happen.

Sasha nervously pulls a brown package out of his coat, and places it carefully in my hand. "I don't know what to do with this—but someone said to give it to— well, maybe you will know what to do with it, or at least if it's meant for you."

The package is roughly the size and shape of a book. Reminded of the time my mother received the letter about Father, I am afraid of what I am about to see.

The handwriting confirms my fears. It appears to be Larissa's, from what I can recall, and it's addressed simply to "Olga and Anna" at this house.

"Thank you," I stammer. "It must be for my mother and me, right?" I yearn to ask Sasha where he picked up the package, but am loathe to make him even more suspicious than he surely must be if he indeed received the package from my sister or someone in Tsarskoe Selo.

As if sensing this reluctance, he says simply, "I know very little. A man handed this to me along with the jewels as payment. He explained nothing except to give me directions. There is no way he could have known I live here now, let alone have any guarantee that I would deliver this."

"Thank you, Comrade," I repeat. "If it is not a package meant for us, I will give it back to you and you can try again to find another 'Olga and Anna.'"

"No problem. Wait. Is that *bread* I smell? My precious wife, are you holding out on me?"

Katya, busy unwrapping her husband's feet and avoiding looking at me, laughs apologetically. "I think I might know something about that. We should get you some rest, though, first."

"No." He kisses her lightly on the forehead. "Bread first. Rest I can get anytime." And they laugh as Katya helps Sasha hobble off to Marina's kitchen, leaving me to fly up the stairs and to my room.

Reluctant to wait for my mother but convinced she would want me to, I sit on the bed and think about Dmitri's eyes—Ivan's eyes—and how they would look at me with disbelief, let alone something between hurt and loathing—if I could just tell him who I *really* am.

Afraid of encountering him, as now I have no idea how to react to his declaration of love and no idea how to get out of this situation, I stay in the room and read all day.

I realize all this reading is an indulgence, and that somebody, somewhere must need my help with something, but besides reading, there is little to do in here except tidy up our now meager belongings, tear and wrap more petticoat bandages, and read more Pushkin.

Packing to go with Dmitri/Ivan, I realize, is futile; it is not, however, as futile as letting him go without us, since that would mean altering the present and hence the past and future.

Instead, I concentrate on my older sister, worrying about what news awaits in the mysterious package.

ℰℐℰℐ

The moment she enters, mother looks at my face and knows something is wrong. "What is it?"

"We received a package. I think it's from Larissa." *Or about her*, I add silently.

"And you didn't open it?"

"I waited for you so we could enjoy it together," I say nervously, and we hug each other before I begin unwrapping the heavy string binding the brown paper.

Prophetically, just before I undo the last string, my mother crosses herself. Inside I find what I should have suspected from the size and width of the package: icons. Specifically, Saint Serafim and the Virgin and child. There is a note slipped between the two frames:

Dear Mama, Papa, and my cherished Olga,
We are fine, but must leave here soon. It is much too dangerous now. I am writing this quickly, as there is little

time. I hope you will find some comfort—or some value—in these last two of my icons. The others we sold for food. We are heading east for now, where P. has some connections. We plan to postpone the wedding a bit longer in the hope that you can join us there in a few months, but only God can tell. We will send word when we can. I pray you are well! God love and protect you both. Give my love to Papa.

Your loving daughter and sister, L.

After reading the note, we take turns tracing the portraits with our fingers. Just as I recall, most of Mary's angelic features are wreathed in silver. Gazing at St. Serafim, with its plainer frame, I feel calmer for some reason.

At last, Mother goes to the bureau and, rewrapping the icons and the note, carefully nestles them beneath some clothing. We wrap our arms around one another, her tears those of regret yet relief, and my own of sadness heightened by the complications of my own situation.

"They will be all right," Mother assures me—and herself. "It is so disturbing, though, that Lara doesn't even know about her father."

"No, Mama. With all she may be going through now, it's better that she retains some hope."

"You're right, of course." She strokes my hair, which has grown stringy and feels flatter and thinner.

I find myself praying that Larissa is still the bright-eyed, optimistic, and slightly plump sister I remember.

Chapter 17

By October Kerensky has not only continued his shuffleboard game with ministerial appointments, but this new head of the provisional government has disbanded and then recalled a new cabinet for the fourth time in the months since he has assumed power. He has become as hated as the former monarchs, with most people agreeing that although he appears to work fifteen-hour days sustained by brandy and morphine, he never actually accomplishes anything. Many have seen him driven around in the former imperial Rolls Royce, and rumors abound that he also brings his mistresses to the former royal bed.

Meanwhile, the ruble has lost three-quarters of its value since the tsar abdicated, and the stock market continues to plunge. The noise outside confirms what the newspapers print: over a million striking factory workers have once again taken to the streets. The latest slogan repeats rhythmically, as if echoing a pounding of the surf: *Peace, land, and bread.*

The waves of protest extend to every minority group, from Muslims to Jews and, of course, those who still own the factories and lands. Those who still have anything to protect cannot hang onto it, and we hear tales of landowners who defend themselves by firing on attacking peasants, only to be run through with pitchforks.

With the exception of the inflation and the daily speculation that we will all have to flee the city and abandon it to the Germans, not much news affects most of us directly—instead, we devote all our time to working, searching for work, scrounging for food and, with the increasingly chilly and rainy days, hunting for firewood.

In spite of how busy the days are, I cannot concentrate on anything but the overwhelming problem in my life: Dmitri. Or Ivan.

Yet even though I devote a substantial amount of energy to avoiding him, we nearly bump into one another one morning just as he hurries in the front door and I have one foot on the bottom of the stairs. Knowing he wasn't due home quite yet, I had started to dash up to what I thought of as my one retreat into solitude and the certainty that I wouldn't have to confront him.

"Dusha," he calls out to me. Dear One. My soul.

Pulling me gently aside, he reaches out as if to embrace me, in spite of the curious looks from tenants lingering around the common area. I take an involuntary step back.

He notices. "What is it?" his fabulous smiles dims for a moment.

When I shake my head mutely, he whispers, "Should we go someplace to talk? It is sleeting once again outside, so maybe here?"

Resigned, I follow him when he takes my hand and leads me to the last place I want to be: his room.

Dmitri—or Ivan—sits on a crate and motions for me to settle on his cot. Yet he can still reach me, and holds out his hands for mine.

"Are you all right?" he asks, concern etched on his handsome features. "Is it your mother? I haven't seen her for days, either."

"No." I could tell him about the package from my sister, but somehow the bigger issue has consumed all my thoughts.

"Then what's the matter, my sweet one?" He pauses then, before asking, "You haven't changed your mind, have you?"

"Yes. I mean no," I mumble quietly.

"Which is it?"

Unable to meet his eyes, I stare at our hands, his firm ink-stained ones stroking mine, and I find myself clasping them tightly.

"It's just that…well, it all seems so sudden. So overwhelming."

"Olga, I know that. And I promise you I would have waited to propose, and ask you to come away with me, if the political situation were not so precarious."

"But we still have a new government," I argue weakly, knowing full well that it will not succeed.

"Yes, we do for now. But based on the articles and speeches I'm printing and editing, I fear that it could topple any day. Kerensky cannot maintain control, and Trotsky has got the people excited about real change—something well beyond what already has changed."

He's not telling me anything I haven't heard recently, but I stall for time. "And you believe Lenin and Trotsky will seize power?"

"I do. There's no doubt Lenin is back now. I understand he's in hiding somewhere in Petrograd, wearing some crazy gray wig and caked on makeup. He's even shaved off that ridiculous goatee."

Encouraging him to keep talking, if for no other reason than to postpone the inevitable conversation about us, I continue to ask questions. "What is going on with the war?"

"We could get bombarded by the Germans from the sea at any time. Lenin fears they could be in our city within a matter of weeks. The one thing I agree with the Bolsheviks on is that they want to get us out of this horrendous war that we cannot win."

"Well, we already lose electricity every night at midnight, not to mention other times, but I understand it's due to the coal shortage."

"Not to mention the almost certainty that the Germans will raid us with those Zeppelin airships if they can see the lights."

In spite of the seriousness of the war threat, I almost smile at this. I know four children from the house who have been stealing devotional candles from the churches for their parents' lighting needs.

"Did you see they are filling barges and trucks with the treasures from the Winter Palace? And the art works from the Hermitage?"

"Thank God, yes." But then he grins. "They also tried filling them with paperwork and government files, but the one from the foreign ministry weighed so much it sunk the barge!"

We laugh together at the image.

"Look!" his eyes twinkle as he unwraps something he has hidden under his jacket.

The aroma gives away the secret before I see it. "Coffee? How is this possible? We cannot get tea!"

"I did what the soldiers are doing today. I hired myself out to some former duke to stand in a queue all day. Well, half the night, too. It cost thirteen rubles for the pound but his ration card would only get one, so he split it with me. Before the war, it was about two rubles per pound. But barely anything is getting through, between the looting of the food trains and then the stores."

"But how will we dare to brew it? Everyone will know!"

"We can distribute tiny cups of it to each of the tenants—or we can bring it with us." At this, something changes in his eyes, and I sense we are done discussing rationing and the war.

"Olga, we must leave now. The mobs are getting more restless. Even the great poet Alexander Blok, who thus far has supported the Bolsheviks, lost his country estate just this week. The hooligans used an ax to demolish his desk, smashed in the library door, stole everything not nailed down and destroyed the rest. And the piano—"

"But they have been doing that for months," I protest weakly.

"Yes, but if Lenin manages to seize power, things will get much, much worse before they improve—if they do improve. He and his Party will transform everything, my dearest, and not for the better."

For some reason I glance around the room, noticing for the first time since he moved in how devoid it is of personal memorabilia. The piano is the one item he will certainly miss. "This Lenin—"

"And Trotsky, and dozens of others who seem to be less bright but more radical."

"They will ruin Russia." I mean for it to come out as a question, but the words come out as a flat statement, as does Dmitri's reply.

"Yes."

"And when, again, do you think this will happen? How much time do we have?"

He tightens his grasp on my hands. "Very little. I'd like to say months, but with the elections coming up in less than two weeks, I suspect Lenin will make a move any day."

"Couldn't we wait until then?" I ask desperately.

"It might be impossible to leave by then," he points out grimly. "Already I think I am being watched more carefully than when I started at the paper."

"But surely the Bolsheviks cannot control everyone!"

"I suspect they will try—and will. So many of us have already left. The nobility, the artists, the writers, the musicians. It is not so difficult now if you have some money to pay people off, at least according to all the information I've gathered."

"But Siberia! Or even Finland or…" I trail off, unable to contemplate all the possibilities. "If we could just wait. Even that couple of weeks."

Dmitri sighs. "I'm trying to explain to you, my love, that it may not be possible to leave at all if we wait. And," he adds earnestly after a few moments, "I don't *want* to wait to be with you!"

His eyes register longing, hope, concern, love, and perhaps fear. "If you don't want to go, Olga, I mean if you have changed your mind, I would try to understand."

Again, I shake my head mutely.

"Is it your mother? Is she refusing to leave Petrograd? I could talk to her."

For an instant, I debate seizing on this excuse, but it will not work: with Father and Lara gone, Anna might feel she no longer has a reason to stay.

"Actually, I have not asked her yet. I need more time to think, Iv—Dmitri."

"Then I will wait for you. I would wait for you forever, Olga."

"But you cannot. It's not safe, I know that."

"No, perhaps not. Yet I'm willing to live through another revolution rather than live without you."

Unable to meet those lovely and loving eyes, I focus on the piano. "You must go," I finally admit reluctantly. "Perhaps, well, perhaps you could return for us in a few months when it is almost over."

"I have thought of that, dearest. But I fear I might not be able to get back to Petrograd—or back into Russia. And how could I leave knowing that you and Anna are in danger?"

I bow my head, letting my thinning hair cover the emotions washing over me in alternating waves of despair and frustration.

For a brief moment, I once again consider confiding in my future great grandfather, telling him that I am Julie, not Olga, a young woman trapped in the wrong time, caught like a prehistoric insect in a globule of amber.

Instead, I let him brush the hair from my face, lift me to my feet, and hold me tightly.

"Just let me think," I whisper as he strokes my hair.

It is at that moment, I believe, that I begin fully to love him as a great grandfather, not a romantic interest. I should warn him. Warn him of everything that will happen.

"I will let you think," he whispers back. "Just remember that I adore you and want more than anything for you to be my wife."

"I won't forget," I murmur into his shoulder, knowing I cannot say more.

And then I flee his room before I break down.

Slipping into bed that night, I sigh deeply. It is too much to hope that any of us will emerge from this revolution the way we were. Many, of course, will end up better off, but all of us will be altered forever by the experience. And once again, I think about the Great-Grandmother Olga I knew and the experiences that must have changed her into a tough, yet compassionate and generous woman. Certainly, she had her bitter moments, and perhaps a strong sense of caution that led her to hoard supplies for the unknown future.

A few hours of tossing and turning later, I realize what must be done.

I am here. I might be stuck in the past for the rest of my—or Olga's—life. I have no right to alter that.

She *must* have left with him, if not now, sometime in

the near future. She did certainly love him with an all-consuming passion.

All I can do is postpone the inevitable.

I will tell Dmitri tomorrow that I *will* go with him, but not for a few days. Although I do not know exactly when my grandmother, or Olga's child, was conceived and born, by my rough calculations, I am quite certain it was in the early 1920s—several years of "breathing" time.

I must live Olga's life as it has unfolded.

Cradling the amber beads, I wish with all my soul that I could talk to Great Grandmother Olga.

Chapter 18

When I awaken, someone else is weeping softly beside me. My mother, I think in a haze, opening my eyes. Yes, there she sits in a straight-backed chair. Her hair is a mess, and she is wearing jeans and a sweatshirt. I have never seen Cheryl look so disheveled.

Cheryl? I sit up quickly, looking around for the first time at what is obviously a hospital room.

I am back! *Hallelujah!*

But then I panic, crying aloud as I remember Dmitri-Ivan and my other mother, Anna.

At my cry, Cheryl leaps out of her chair and comes to where I am hooked to an IV and propped on an elevated bed.

"You're awake! Darling, you're awake, aren't you?"

"Of course, moth—Cheryl."

"No, darling. 'Mother' is fine. It's the word I've waited to hear for weeks!"

"Weeks?" I demand incredulously.

"Well, over two weeks."

"Mother! Please tell me what you're talking about. What has happened?"

"You mean since we found you passed out in the little room off Olga's bedroom?"

She strokes my hair and reaches to hand me a glass of water. "Of course, the doctors said this might happen. That you might not remember much, but we don't know exactly what caused the coma, my darling. I'm only grateful that you're alive and apparently healthy. "You don't remember what happened in that room, sweetheart? Did you hit your head?"

Between sips of water, I manage to convey that I remember almost nothing. Yet I do. I remember every single thing that happened to me in the past.

"Todd found you. He called the ambulance, but you haven't regained consciousness at all since then," Cheryl said.

None of this is possible. None of it makes sense. I know I didn't fall unconscious or have some elaborate dream. I know I've been gone nearly a year—not just over two weeks—and been living in 1917 Russia. I know I fell in love with Dmitri/Ivan and that now I've lost him forever, and he wasn't mine anyways and the whole thing was, well, almost a disaster for the present.

"Where are my beads?" I interrupt suddenly.

"What beads? I checked in all your clothes and belongings myself."

"I was holding or wearing an amber necklace." Then I touch my chest and feel it under my hospital gown. "This one!"

"Wherever did you get that? You weren't wearing it before, I can assure you. And the nurses should certainly have removed it!"

But I am not listening to her.

If I stroke the beads, will they take me back?

I close my eyes and wait. As relieved as I am to see my real mother, I want her to think I am asleep again so I can think. Can sort all this out. Can weigh my options.

Should I go back? Could I go back? Do I really want to go back? The thought of Ivan brings fresh tears, although I remember then what I had just realized before I returned to the present: that he was my great-grandfather, meaning off limits to Julie Myers, but not to Olga. Did he, Olga, and Anna escape via Finland? Did they find happiness? Of course, they must have, since Cheryl and I are here. They had a child who had a child who gave birth to my mother who gave birth to me.

I struggle to figure it all out. They must have left Petrograd and then eventually left Russia. But why? What happened to Anna Ivanovna and to Larissa?

"Julie? Pumpkin, are you fading away on us?"

I open my eyes again and try to sit up. I need to get out of bed and get answers. "Mother!" I know I startle her. "Grandma Olga's stuff. Where is it? Did you toss everything away? What about the house?"

Apparently so relieved I am awake and cognizant of my identity and surroundings, she has forgotten that I awoke wearing a mysterious necklace. Cheryl smiles for the first time. "Don't worry, my pet. We postponed getting rid of everything when you were ill. I've been working on some of it myself—and believe it or not, I think I'm having a good time. And then when we found you weren't going to wake up for who knows how long, Fred and I moved our things from the motel to the house and waited for you to return to us."

"Fred is here?"

"Yes, Fred is here—and worried sick. But the bottom line is that Great Grandma Olga's things are waiting for you, just as her will specified."

"Then can you get me out of here?" I point distastefully at the tubes taped to my fingers and arm, but as if on cue, a nurse enters and smiles.

"Shall we try some real food? Some broth?" she asks, and I nod, albeit somewhat impatiently.

I want to get back to the house. I want to try to find some answers.

∽∾∽

It rapidly becomes apparent that no one is going to let me go anywhere until I am probed and poked, and until I have yet another MRI.

They keep me "for observation" three more days, but at last Cheryl announces that the hospital has discharged me and that "Fred has been staying at the house and getting it ready for us. We thought it would make more sense for you to recover there."

I feel fine, however. As Fred's car pulls up the driveway, I almost feel as if I were coming home. The house no longer seems drab to me, but almost magical. Perhaps not as elaborate as the palaces and mansions in Petrograd, but spacious and splendid just the same. I can see why, with its turrets and Queen Anne style, it would have appealed to Grandma Olga.

Inside, my eyes sweep the parlor. The organ. It makes sense now that she would've kept it even though she didn't play. It would have been Ivan's. I run my fingers almost lovingly over the carved figurines that decorate the wood, remembering "my" Dmitri playing the piano in the recital room where he lived in 1917.

Upstairs is the photograph of the two of them, and I stroke the now very familiar faces. Ivan looks several years older than I remember, but just as handsome. I wish I could talk to him, to explain the truth about who I am—or was—before, like Alice, I woke up to find that Wonderland—with all its wonders yet horrors—had all been some kind of dream.

Except it hadn't. I know I was there, and, apparently, I did not interfere so much with the past that it altered the present.

Cheryl—mother—busies herself making coffee. "I'll have tea," I announce, and she looks at me as if I have lost my mind. I laugh. "I just prefer it now."

I am grateful to see that Fred has moved my luggage to Grandma Olga's room.

The storage room is closed and locked, but someone has left the key next to Grandma Olga's atomizers on the oak dresser. Inside the once mysterious little room, everything is as I remember. My mother and Fred must not have paid any attention to the empty lacquer box. The love seat on which I once curled up and ended up in the past is just as I left it, and I struggle to remember anything about my apparent abandonment of it. Because regardless of what my 1990s body was doing, the real me definitely left. The beads prove that, or at least I believe they do, since they apparently went with me. But I have had days to adapt to the idea that I may never understand exactly what happened.

It is then that I recognize the icon: St. Serafim. It has to be the same one, right down to the bear, the golden halo, and the crucifix. But the Virgin and baby are missing, and I wonder if Larissa returned to reclaim it or if Olga sold it for money—in Russia or in Michigan.

"Exquisite, isn't it?" Cheryl says behind me. "I never saw it before."

"None of this stuff?"

"Some of it, yes. I remembered it when I came in here a week or so ago. Grandma used to let me play with the nested dolls, but the rock collection was my favorite. Especially the amber and the lapis lazuli. But knowing how much I loved amber, I can't figure out why I never saw that necklace before—you know, the one you said you found in the palekh box. The lacquered box."

I don't reply, and she walks inside and picks up the box, lovingly stroking its cover.

She sighs deeply. "I'm ashamed of a lot of things, honey. If I hadn't practically cursed my grandmother out just because we were Russians, perhaps many of the tensions we had between us wouldn't have happened. I hated my heritage."

"I just thought it was silly," I admit. "But I didn't go through what either of you did. You must have been a tough little girl, Mom."

"Not as tough as Olga. But perhaps that's why we clashed so much, too. I was a mean little girl sometimes after my parents died. I didn't want to be here, but I didn't really want to be anywhere without them."

We sit together on the love seat. The amber beads rest on the bureau, but I do not dare touch them. For a long time we are both silent.

"I don't think it's silly anymore," I say finally.

"What isn't?"

"Being Russian. I love that I am—or at least that my

ancestors were. I'm planning to do some research on the family tree, if you don't go all ballistic on me, Mom."

Cheryl laughs. Actually laughs. "Research to your heart's content, my dear. I have a confession to make."

"Which is?"

"That I had two long weeks in this house to go through things and reacquaint myself with memories—or maybe reacquaint myself with myself would be more accurate. In spite of all the worry about losing you, I found time to have tea from the samovar and look at old pictures and just plain reminisce about some of the really great things that my grandparents did for me. Besides—" She winks. "—these days it really is kind of cool to be Russian."

"But are you still mad at Olga?"

"No, not really, honey. I didn't understand her most of the time, but I know that deep down I loved her. It just took me a lot of fear of losing you and a lot of time browsing this house to figure that out."

So I tell her.

Not that I traveled back into the past, because I doubt even my own mother would believe that when she'd been staring at my comatose body for weeks, but what I know about Great Grandmother Olga. "I had this long dream about the past while I was 'out,'" I begin.

And then I share a good deal of it with her—as theories that unravel Olga's life the way her mother and I once separated threads from old socks to modify our gowns into something more simple, I talk for a long time, struggling to explain what I know of her life back then. Why Cheryl's grandmother and my great grandmother valued her privacy and didn't want to share her house with strangers. Why she hoarded things in case of shortages or another war. Why she didn't worry what people thought of who she was. Why her cultural heritage meant so much to her.

"You got all that from a dream?" Cheryl demands. "Surely Olga must have told you that she once shared her home with a dozen or so families."

"Well, maybe she did tell me some of it when I was young," I lie.

"I will be damned. Humph." Cheryl gets up to get us some more tea, but then turns back. "That does explain a lot. And do you know what I think?"

"What?"

"That we're Russian-Americans, you and me, kid. That's just what is, and I guess I'm glad of it now. I just wish your great grandmother was still here for me to tell her so many things." For a moment, I imagine I see tears on her unmade up face, but Cheryl leaves the tiny, once secret room before I can be certain.

I have my own wishes, like being able to say goodbye to my—or to Olga's—family. Like trying to find out more about them. Well, I might not be able to do a thing about the first one, but I can the second.

Chapter 19

O ver the next week, I continue to deal with a very attentive mother and stepfather. I am aided in my attempts to get rid of some local reporters curious about the mysterious coma and a few well-meaning neighbors by Cheryl, who reminds me of Great Grandma Olga when she all but slams the door—or at least firmly shuts it—in their faces. In her new, fiercely protective role, she won't even go to the store unless Fred stays with me.

At last, I am able to get back to the packing, although it takes days before anyone will let me leave the house and go where I really want to be: the library.

The local library is smaller than the one where I worked, and, without borrowing privileges, I am limited to sitting on a couch near the window and reading textbooks about Lenin's revolution. It sounds as if it turned out as awful as I had feared, although admittedly it evolved into a much fairer system for people like Katya, Sasha, and Marina. In the end, the revolutionaries turned out to be nothing but a "pack of cards," which toppled the first time Mikhail Gorbachev began to push for the return of people's freedoms.

"You might want to try the library at Michigan State," the woman shelving books in the history section suggests the second time I come in.

Early the next morning, I talk Cheryl into letting me borrow the car to head for East Lansing. Its library overwhelms me at first, but enables me to start a genealogical search. Tiffany, as well as my other friends in Texas, would think I am daft, buried all day in a university library looking for evidence of my ancestors. I laugh when I remember how Tiffany and I used to moan and groan over library assignments.

However, I find nothing, even with access to a computer, that tells me what happened to my sister and mother—Grandma Olga's sister and mother—and in the end I drive the hour back, heat up the samovar, and sip tea from one of the floral patterned tea cups in the china cabinet.

Cheryl joins me on the wrap-around porch, and together we listen to frogs and crickets singing somewhere beyond the lilac bushes.

"It's beautiful here," she murmurs unexpectedly.

I am nearly too shocked to respond. "It is, isn't it?" I say finally.

"When I was growing up," she explains, "I never noticed. Now that I've toured a good part of the world, I can appreciate some of what I left behind. Although, believe it or not, Fred wants to take me to Russia next summer!"

My mother has changed as much as I have, that much is obvious. Perhaps my apparent near death shocked her more than I could have expected, but at last, she seems like a real mother. I turn to look at her, smiling at the sight of her blue jeans and tee shirt, although I notice that her lipstick matches the shirt.

"I'm amazed." I force a smile. I *am* surprised, but find myself jealous, as well. Since my return from the past, I've realized that the new passion I have found for the land of my ancestors has only deepened—not to mention the feelings I've discovered within myself about my family. "Mom, did you know Great Grandma Olga had an older sister?"

Cheryl's forehead wrinkles into a series of puzzle pieces for a moment, and I realize for the second time this week she is wearing no foundation, concealer, blush, or face powder. Only the lipstick. "Yes! Yes, I did know that, pumpkin. I had almost forgotten."

"Do you know what happened to her?" I ask eagerly. After days of searching for answers, perhaps they are right in front of me.

"No, I don't." She leans back with her coffee and stares up at the trellis for a few moments. "Let's see. I seem to remember Grandma talking about her quite a bit when I was little. I used to complain because I didn't have a sister or brother, and she would tell me stories about herself and—oh, drat, I forgot her name—"

"Lara?"

"Yes, that was it. How did you know?" But she rushes on now, as if releasing a netful of memories as delicate and delightful as butterflies. "Olga and Lara used to go on the swings together, do fancy embroidery, shop in St. Petersburg, eat some kind of sweet Easter bread—oh, what was that called—never mind. They even went to grand balls where they waltzed with royalty! Or so she said then, and I guess I never completely believed her. She told me so many fairytales, too, about princesses and firebirds and golden apples. I think it all ran together into one fantastical storybook life. But I was a very practical child. I suppose I only half listened."

"You actually didn't believe her?"

"Well, I believed she once had a sister, although I don't think I was curious enough to ask about her. I was kind of a selfish kid, not to mention too wrapped up in my parents' death, and didn't really worry about my grandmother."

She seems to have forgotten her coffee, and once again, I imagine a tear in my mother's eyes that may, or may not, be leaking from her mascara-free eyelashes.

"Now that I think about it, I guess taking me in must have been as hard on her as it was on me."

"Maybe she did what she thought was best for you," I offer quietly.

"I don't doubt that now. None of us ever makes as good of a parent as we think we will be. I know that, honey. When it comes to you, I haven't always been—"

"It's okay, Mother. I know you have had your own problems and needs. But you're here now." Somehow, I don't feel at all magnanimous saying this, only realizing its truth at the moment. In her own way, Cheryl is as strong as Anna was, and I yearn to tell her every detail of the life I led as her own great grandmother Anna Sheretno.

Maybe someday I will try to pick up the strands of the story.

"Anyway," my mother reaches for her coffee and absentmindedly brushes a ladybug off her jeans. "I think Olga said she searched for Lara for years and years. She almost found her once in England, but somehow World War II interfered and she lost that link. I believe my grandfather also tried to find her during the war, but then he got stationed in the Pacific."

"Dmitri—I mean Ivan, Great Grandfather Ivan, fought in World War II?"

"Yes, he did. He was way too old to get drafted, but he insisted on going and fighting for his new country. He got shot in the leg, though, and about once in a week he'd have a shot of vodka to celebrate that it hadn't been in his arm or hand. He was a pianist and an organist, you know."

"I know," I whisper.

Cheryl—Mother—smiles at me and then frowns. "You know, my grandparents must have had an awful life, between the Revolution, fleeing the country, getting started here—and then the Depression and the War."

"Not to mention losing their only child—and my grandparents."

"And her sister. But wars separate people, sometimes forever. I wonder if there is even a slim chance Lara is still alive. Somehow I suspect grandmother clung to that hope, but I might be wrong. I know that she told me her mother died of some disease before they left Russia…"

Anna gone. Of course. They all were. Once again, I almost wish I could wear the amber beads back into the past and say goodbye to everyone.

When I am silent for a long time, listening to the birds and thinking about Petrograd/Petersburg, my mother finally interrupts.

"Where do you go, honey? When you get so silent?"

"Just thinking about the past. I guess I never took much interest in it before, did I?"

"No, but then neither did I. It's a mistake I plan to remedy. We can learn a lot about the past. *You* already have. I'd especially like to go to Russia and speak with people who had to build a new future to undo its mistakes and forget about its heartaches."

"And maybe now that so many records are being opened in Russia, I could do a real genealogical search!" I am excited now, although I have no idea how to go about it after my failed fledgling attempt. "And if I learn Russian, I could try to go over there, too!"

"Would you like to stay?" my mother asks suddenly.

"In Russia?" For a moment, I am confused, as if my mother knows something.

"No, in Michigan. In this house."

"But how is that even possible? The house will belong to the shelter soon."

"Fred wants to buy it from them for us," she says simply.

"But I thought you hated it here."

"I admit the bad childhood memories may never go away," she says slowly, biting at her lipstick. "Don't forget that I grew up during the McCarthy Era, when everyone who even uttered the name of Russia or the Soviet Union—or knew someone who did—was ostracized or even arrested. Your grandfather actually lost his job as a furniture designer, and that's no small feat here in the Furniture Capital of the World. Especially when you were a decorated war veteran. His patents actually were very popular, but his thick Russian accent and immigrant status, even though he became an American citizen, made everyone suspect him. And my entire family. But now I realize I have good memories, too."

"I had forgotten."

"Forgotten what?"

"That Great Grandpa Ivan made furniture." But I had not forgotten that Dmitri did, and for the fortieth time since I've been back in the present I feel like bawling.

"Of course, you know he designed and made nearly all the furniture in the house. Except the organ. That's one reason your great-grandmother would never remodel or get rid of any of it. It *is* good quality work, and I don't know if my own father would've ever been that talented if he'd lived. He worked in the same factory, but in manufacturing."

"So then all this—" I wave behind me at the house full of ornate mahogany and blond pine and oak furniture with fancy scrolls and carvings that, now that I look at it, remind me of nights watching Dmitri carve pieces for the tenants. "But surely he made decent money doing that?"

"Yes, I believe there were some patents he sold," Cheryl answers thoughtfully. "In fact, saving up some of that money may be how my grandmother had money to donate to others."

"How did they get here, Mother? To the States?"

"I don't know much about it, Julie. Only that they left through Finland, then England, where my grandmother may have had some family. I also know they lived in New York for a while, where my grandfather got his start in the furniture business. I think that's the reason they settled in West Michigan after the Depression. There was no work for him in New York. Goodness, you've got me thinking about things I'd forgotten for decades!"

"Cheryl—Mother, did you ever come across another icon, one of the Virgin and infant Jesus surrounded by silver plate? In Olga's things, I mean."

"No, I don't think so. Well, maybe." She stands up to refill our cups and then pauses to look at me. "But until you were ill I never paid a lot of attention to the things in this house, dear. I'm sorry now for all the questions I never asked, but it's too late now to ask them."

I know exactly how she feels, which is why the next morning at breakfast, I encourage my mother to tell me about the air raid drills during the Cuban Missile crisis.

"Well, they were terrifying, Julie, but beyond that there isn't a lot to tell. When the sirens blared, they never let us know whether it was a drill or if the Soviets actually were coming to take over. I was still in grade school and too far away from home to get there—and we didn't have a bomb shelter—so I had to dash to someone else's house to hide. It seems as if we only had five minutes to get there—maybe ten. I used to fly, as if my feet were scissors opening and closing as widely as possible. Yet, somehow, my classmates always looked at me as if I were the one responsible for everything. I've told you, honey, I couldn't get out of this town fast enough."

"But didn't you want to stay where you spent your childhood with your parents?"

My mother sighs. It is not a subject she has brought up often in my childhood. "I suppose I was afraid to. Too many bad things happened here. And to this day I never go to Lake Michigan. It's just too disturbing to think of the way the waves swallowed up my parents." Her voice cracks as she says the last sentence.

"And yet you're sure we can actually stay here now? The memories won't be too much for you?" I'm not sure I would've even thought to ask that question BAB— Before the Amber Beads—nor that her answer would have mattered to me. But I don't want my mother to be unhappy, even though she has assured me already that there are countless opportunities here for her designer business.

"And lots of antiques," she had added the other day. "I'm absolutely fine with staying in this area. And Russians are 'in' right now, so to speak, as I mentioned before. Perhaps in a few years no one younger than me will even remember that they were once considered the Bad Guys. Are *you* sure you want to live here?"

"I think so, but I won't know for sure until we just do it." And I really *don't* know. Will staying here instead of going back to my old life in Texas make me any happier? Or will I stay rooted in the more distant past, a place and time I am still having trouble tearing my thoughts away from?

But yet in so many ways it seems right. Living in Great Grandma Olga's house. Going to school amidst the corn fields and gently rolling hills. "Taking tea" each afternoon after school on the porch. Perhaps this is where I am meant to be. Perhaps someday this is where I will meet my own Ivan.

"Maybe I could apply to Michigan State this fall," I mention hesitantly, already planning to talk to Todd. "The librarian there told me they have an excellent Russian program."

Cheryl looks surprised, but instead of dismissing my idea, as she would have a few months ago, she nods. "Good plan. There will be lots of opportunities there now that Yeltsin is in power and Russia is evolving into a democratic state."

So much for Cheryl's distaste for her ancestry, although at least I comprehend the reasons behind it now. Then, too, she admitted that weeks surrounded by Grandma Olga's icons and memories have changed her. I know that they have changed me, and that, in some way, I am spiritually linked not only to Olga, but to my heritage.

It occurs me later that day that there is something I must do: I will go to a jeweler and have several beads removed from the necklace. Like the sea maiden who has lost her loved ones, I plan to scatter some amber on the graves of Olga and Ivan. And somehow I feel sure that Olga would approve of me burying some pieces beside my own grandparents' headstones.

"Are you sure you've never seen this necklace before?" I ask Cheryl again, removing the amber beads from my pocket where I bravely placed them this morning.

She picks the necklace up and strokes its beads, and suddenly I find myself terrified that she will disappear right out of Websterville and plunge back into early twentieth-century Russia.

"No, I still don't think so. And these just weren't the kind of beads that were popular in my day." She hands the necklace back. "But it is yours, Julie. Olga loved you and she probably loved me. I think I just disappointed her when I refused to listen to her Russian tales and share her interest in our heritage." She heaves a big sigh. "I know now that I was wrong, but like I told you yesterday, it is difficult to think of anyone but yourself when you are a seven-year-old orphan. But guess what?"

My mother's new, animated self is kind of cool, I decide. "What?"

"I think my mother—and your grandmother—was Ukrainian, not Russian! I found some old newspaper articles about the drowning, and one of the them said she had immigrated from there."

"Really?"

"Well, I need to dig a little more, but maybe my own search will help both of us find some answers to the questions of our past. "

"I hope so."

But as new as my pleasure and curiosity about the past are, I know I have to concentrate on the present, too.

Upstairs I run bubble bath into a warm tub before sinking into it. Ah, what luxury. *Almost* I can believe nothing ever happened to me. Of course, I still have plenty of adhesive marks on my body from the electrodes hooked up to me during my alleged coma. But suddenly my raised knees catch my attention. It's there. I finger the scar on my left knee, and know I got it in 1917. I was hauling wood around in the house I shared first with my parents and Lara, and then with Katya and Sasha and Dmitri.

I'm not crazy. I wasn't comatose. Just as I've believed ever since my "return," I really did spend nearly an entire year in revolutionary Russia. The thought, however, doesn't make me giddy or worried. Instead, I feel a sense of satisfaction tinged with the sadness that I may never know about the ensuing years in Great Grandmother Olga's life.

But the satisfaction comes from knowing she was a survivor. Both she and Ivan. I am proud to be their descendant.

Slipping into my robe, I decide to put the amber necklace lying on my dresser away for good. Wearing it every day is risky if I don't want to end up suddenly back in Lenin's Soviet Union. I keep the door to the closet unlocked now, since it is all mine. Inside, I have carefully placed St. Serafim's icon next to the photograph of Olga and a much older Ivan. I don't want to look at them too often, as I know that I have to get on with my own future.

Lifting the lid of the lacquer firebird box, I start to place the beads inside. I notice for the first time, however, that the box is lined with a piece of folded paper.

Curiously, I slide it out. It contains a hand-written list, and for a moment, I regret having lost all my Russian language abilities with my return to the present. But the lettering is English, not Cyrillic.

Sergei Ivanovich Sheretno1875-1917
Anna Petrovna Sheretno 1880-1918
Larissa Sergeievna Sheretno 1897-??
Olga Sergeievna Kuznentsov 1899-
Ivan Igorovich Kuznetsov 1895-1969
Peter Ivanovich Kuznetsov1929-1959
Ekaterina Petrovna Kuznetsov 1952-

I cannot help it. I cry for Anna, my "mother," who may have succumbed to typhoid. For my "father," who died fighting in a war for which an entire nation was inadequately equipped and poorly led. I cry for my "sister," who apparently disappeared into the flames of the past. For the great grandfather I came to know when he was a handsome, earnest young man. For the grandfather and grandmother I never knew. For friends like Sasha and Katya who may or may not have survived.

How could Grandma Olga, who knew and loved

them all, have lived with so much heartache and loss?

No, there is no way to imagine what she felt all these years, not knowing Larissa's fate, yet realizing she herself could not return to her homeland to search. Perhaps, from the comments she made, she did not want to go back to a place that took everyone she loved from her. As tenacious and generous as she was, she and Ivan must have clung to one another for all the decades they had together. I can imagine her sitting on the veranda, drinking tea and listening to him play the organ inside their spacious house. Watching the free spaces out beyond, where people could live the way they wanted.

She must've found peace, after all. Lived out her life without fear of a knock at the door or her identify being discovered. Without sharing her house with strangers.

Glancing out at a flock of sparrows fluttering above corn and pumpkin fields, I can sense that same peace. The kind that comes with knowing you've come home at last.

THE END

AUTHOR'S NOTE

In late October of 1917 (November based on the rest of the world's adoption of the Gregorian calendar and Russia's continued use of the Julian, which was thirteen days behind), Lenin and his Bolsheviks stormed the Winter Palace, overthrowing the provisional government in a second revolution. This sparked a civil war that lasted several years, during which Lenin nationalized government, industry, agriculture, and education. He also ended Russia's involvement in World War I. The tsar, tsaritsa, and their five children were executed in Ekaterinburg—by most accounts on Lenin's orders—in July 1918.

Although atrocities and mass executions were committed on all sides, Lenin and then Stalin *did* manage forcibly to transform a backward society in which only the privileged few profited into one in which most people had increased opportunities, education, and a somewhat more equitable role in their own country. In spite of the fact that the Communist system Lenin envisioned fell apart during the late 1980s and early 1990s, the USSR (Russia was renamed the Union of Soviet Socialist Republics during the Communist Era) made dramatic economic, scientific, and military strides in the seven decades following 1917.

Like Larissa and Pavel, many people disappeared from

all official records during the period in which the novel is set and in ensuring years. Some were executed, others went into hiding and/or assumed new identities, and still others managed to flee the country and go into exile throughout the world. Former aristocrats who stayed in Russia often were treated as threats to the government, and some families became separated forever, with no idea what had happened to their loved ones.

Although I have made every effort possible to ensure accuracy in my portrayals of the last days of the tsarist and the early days of the revolutionary periods, some license has been taken (with for instance, the imagined reception at the Winter Palace that Olga/Julie attends when she first enters the past). Nor do I know for certain that "tents" were set up in the Summer Gardens and around the Admiralty during the period from February to the autumn of 1917. However, homelessness was rampant then and after Lenin assumed power, and throughout this period and the civil war that followed, masses of people were displaced or left the front and thousands poured into the city of Petrograd/Petersburg/Leningrad from throughout the country. Thus I based that description on a similar "tent city" that I saw set up near the Kremlin by homeless people from various republics when the Soviet Union broke into separate states in the early 1990s and emerged as the Russian Federation.

As noted above, in most cases I've followed the "old" Julian calendar dates still utilized during the months in which the novel takes place (the newer Gregorian calendar—13 days ahead--had long been in use in most other parts of the world). Hence some difficulties occur when researching due to this calendar disparity, as well as the difference between when specific holidays such as Christmas and Easter are celebrated in the Western Christian vs. Eastern Orthodox churches. For instance, even first-person accounts differ on specific dates for the ceremonies surrounding Orthodox Holy Week and Easter in 1917, depending on the culture and even religious affiliation of the primary witness or the researcher.

In spite of consulting numerous sources, I also often found it challenging to obtain details regarding how the peasants lived during these months (although lives of the aristocracy and key revolutionaries are well documented). Similarly, I frequently encountered conflicting accounts and information. To take just another example, some sources claim it was bitterly cold when the women workers marched through Petrograd, but a couple others insist the city was enjoying a brief warm spell.

Any and all remaining errors or misconceptions are my own.

Websterville is a fictional small town set outside the (real) city of Grand Rapids, Michigan. All other locations mentioned in the U.S. and Russia are actual places.

Key Works Consulted
(and further recommended reading)

"Alexander Palace Time Machine."
<www.alexanderpalace.org>.

Bergamini, John D. *The Tragic Dynasty: A History of the Romanovs*. Old Saybrook, CT: Konecky & Konecky, 1969.

Cowles, Virginia. *The Romanovs*. NY: Harper & Row, 1971, Crawford, Rosemary and Donald. *Michael and Natasha*. NY: Avon Books, 1997

"Easter in Russia, Ukraine, and Easter Europe." *The Mendeleyev Journal*. Online.
https://russianreport.wordpress.com/religion-in-russia/easter-in-russia

Erickson, Caroline. *Alexandra: The Last Tsarina*. NY: St. Martin's Press, 2001.

Gelardi, Julia P. *From Splendor to Revolution: The Romanov Women, 1847-1928*. NY: St. Martin's Press, 2011.

Kelly, Laurence, ed. *A Traveller's Companion to St. Petersburg*. Brooklyn: Interlink Books, 2003.

King, Greg and Penny Wilson. *The Resurrection of the Romanovs: Anastasia, Anna Anderson, and the World's Greatest Royal Mystery*. Hoboken, NJ: John Wiley & Sons: 2011.

Lambton, Lord Antony. *Elizabeth and Alexandra*. NY: E. P. Dutton, 1985

Lawrence, John. *A History of Russia*, 7th ed. NY: Meridian, 1993.

Mazanik, Anna. "Final Months of Peace: Russia on the Eve of the First World War." *Russian Life* 57, No. 4 (July/August 2014). 29-34.

McKean, Robert B. *St. Petersburg Between the Revolutions*. New Haven: Yale University Press, 1990.

Moynahan, Brian. *Comrades: 1917—Russia in Revolution*. Boston: Little, Brown, & Co., 1992.

Riasanovsky, Nicholas V. *A History of Russia*, 4th ed. NY: Oxford University Press, 1984.

Salisbury, Harrison E. *Black Night, White Snow: Russia's Revolutions: 1905-1917*. NY: Doubleday, 1977.

Sherrow, Victoria. *Life During the Russian Revolution.* San Diego: Lucent Books, 1998.

Smith, Douglas. *Former People: The Final Days of the Russian Aristocracy.* NY: Farrar, Strauss, & Giroux, 2012.

Steinberg, Mark D. and Vladimir M. Khrustalev. *The Fall of the Romanovs.* Some documents trans. Elizabeth Tucker. New Haven & London: Yale University Press, 1995. 137-146.

Troyat, Henri. *Daily Life in Russia Under the Last Tsar.* Trans. Malcolm Barnes. Stanford, CA: Stanford University Press, 1982.

About the Author

Judith A. Rypma, who teaches Children's and Young Adult literature at Western Michigan University, is also a well-known poet and Russian Studies expert who has just completed her twenty-fifth trip to Russia. Her previous poetry collections include *Looking for the Amber Room*, *Amber Notes*, and *Worshipping at Lenin's Mausoleum*. *Amber Beads* is her first published novel.